Best Irish Short Stories

Best
Irish Short Stories

Edited by
DAVID MARCUS

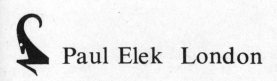
Paul Elek London

800327

Published 1976 by Elek Books Limited
54-58 Caledonian Road
London N1 9RN

ISBN 0 236 40032 0

Printed in Great Britain by Biddles Limited, Guildford

Contents

Acknowledgments

'Tell Me Once Again You Love Me' by Vincent Lawrence first appeared in *Transatlantic Review,* Spring 1975; 'A Cow in the House' by Benedict Kiely in the *Dublin Magazine,* Summer 1973; 'Arrival' by Edward Brazil in *Icarus,* Winter 1974; 'Compassion' by Ita Daly in *The Irish Times,* 16 January 1975; 'Water from the Well' by Brian Power in *The Arts in Ireland,* 1974. The following stories were first published in 'New Irish Writing' *(The Irish Press)*: 'The Heel of the Hunt', by John A. Ryan, 3 August 1974; 'Skin' by Neil Jordan, 1 February 1975; 'Banished Misfortune' by Dermot Healy, 5 April 1975. Acknowledgments are due to the Editors of all the above publications.

Notes on Authors

PATRICK BOYLE: Born in County Antrim. A retired bank manager, he now lives outside Dublin. Two collections of stories, *At Night All Cats are Grey* and *All Looks Yellow to the Jaundiced Eye,* and a novel, *Like Any Other Man,* have placed him in the forefront of contemporary Irish writers.

EDWARD BRAZIL: Born Dublin 1954. He is currently an Arts student in Trinity College, Dublin. His first story, which was published in 'New Irish Writing', won a Hennessy Literary Award in 1975.

IAN COCHRANE: Born in County Antrim 1941. He moved to London in 1960. He has published three highly praised novels about Protestant working-class life in Northern Ireland — *In the Country of the Skin, Gone in the Head* and *Jesus on a Stick.*

ITA DALY: Born County Leitrim 1944. She is a teacher in Dublin. A Hennessy Literary Award winner in 1972 and *The Irish Times* Short Story Award winner of 1975. Her work has also appeared in *Threshold* and in *The Critic* (USA).

DERMOT HEALY: Born County Westmeath 1947. He won a Hennessy Literary Award in 1974.

JOHN JORDAN: Born Dublin 1930 and educated at University College, Dublin and Oxford. His poetry — *Patrician Stations* and *A Raft from Flotsam* — and critical essays have appeared widely in Ireland.

NEIL JORDAN: Born Dublin 1951. His work has appeared in 'New Irish Writing' and *Stand.*

BENEDICT KIELY: Born County Tyrone 1919. A frequent contributor to the *New Yorker,* he is one of Ireland's most highly regarded writers and critics. His novels are: *Land Without Stars, In a Harbour Green, Call for a Miracle, Honey Seems Bitter, There was an Ancient House,*

The Cards of the Gambler, The Captain with the Whiskers, Dogs Enjoy the Morning. He has also published a collection of short stories, *A Journey to the Seven Streams.*

VINCENT LAWRENCE: Born Wexford 1940. A Hennessy Literary Award winner in 1971; his first novel *An End to Flight* won the Robert Pitman Award in 1973. He taught for five years in Nigeria and is now back teaching in Dublin.

BRYAN MacMAHON: Born County Kerry 1909. Recently retired after a lifetime of teaching, he is one of Ireland's leading short story writers.

SEAN MacMATHUNA: Born County Kerry 1936. He is a teacher in Dublin. He has published a number of stories in Irish and has contributed English language stories to 'New Irish Writing'.

BRIAN POWER: Born Dublin 1930. He was ordained in 1958 and is currently doing a Master's course in Social Work in Boston. He has published a number of stories in Ireland and in 1973 won a Hennessy Literary Award.

JOHN A. RYAN: Born in Waterford. He has published one story in 'New Irish Writing' which won him a Hennessy Literary Award in 1975.

EITHNE STRONG: Born County Limerick 1923. She has published many stories and poems in Irish periodicals.

MAURA TREACY: Born County Kilkenny 1946. She has published stories and articles widely in Ireland and in 1974 won the Writers' Week in Listowel Short Story Award.

The Hennessy Literary Awards were instituted in 1971 and are given annually for the best short stories by new Irish writers published in *The Irish Press* weekly 'New Irish Writing' page. The judges have been: 1971, Elizabeth Bowen and William Trevor; 1972, Brian Friel and James Plunkett; 1973, Kingsley Amis and Sean O'Faolain; 1974, Edna O'Brien and V.S. Pritchett; 1975, William Saroyan and Brian Moore.

The Writers' Week in Listowel is an annual festival of writers in County Kerry, in connection with which a national Short Story Competition is held.

Introduction

Not very long ago we were constantly being told that the novel was dying; and to all intents and purposes, death — hastened no doubt by the severe economic depression of recent years — duly took place. The emaciated shade of its former self that nowadays occasionally appears is evidence only that though dead, the novel will not lie down.

The opposite is the case with the modern short story: here the death-watch was reported years ago, the mourners have long fallen silent, and today the grave is virtually deserted — yet the short story is not dead, only lying down.

The novel, of course, depended solely on the hardback publisher — maim the publisher and you kill the novel; the short story depended mainly on the periodical — kill off practically all the literary periodicals and most of the women's and general periodicals which included one or more stories in their contents, and you throw the short story back for survival onto its last line of defence, the beleaguered book publishers and the literary press.

At this point I must hasten to emphasize that I am referring only to the English-language story written by British and Irish authors. The state of the short story in the USA may afford no cause for complacency but it is rather more encouraging than in these islands. And that this is, and always has been, the case is of vital importance to the Irish short story. For the fact is that the Irish short story is not dead or dying or more noticeably comatose than before — it has always been alive and well, but has lived (i.e. obtained its livelihood) almost exclusively in exile.

Now for a literary form thus doubly disadvantaged — an ostensibly regional expression of an already limited-appeal medium — to have survived in this way since early this century argues a number of virtues: a continuing dedication on the part of its practitioners, a universality which enables readers of widely differing backgrounds and cultures the better to know themselves, and some special indefinable charm that is both inimitable and renewable; the lot, of course, crafted with a consummate technique that satisfies the highest standards of its host editors and publishers.

But at the same time as these virtues are the key to the réclame which the Irish short story has enjoyed for so long, they are also useful pointers towards explaining a more philosophical question: why the Irish writer's obsession with the short story in the first place?

Ireland is a small country, with a small population which lacked a developed visual sense and a sophisticated ear and to whose always-restricted mental and physical horizons the miniaturization and particularization of the short story have a natural appeal. And with a strongly rooted bardic tradition, the story vied with the poem as a medium both of entertainment and of social history. Indeed in Ireland, where there is no novel tradition, the short story is the repository of a rich store of social history. Then there is the Irish penchant for over-elaboration – a penchant which can manifest itself in the adjectival orgasms of much Irish writing from Gaelic poetry to O'Caseyed prose, in the ritualized glory of the Book of Kells, in the tranced convolvulus of *Finnegans Wake;* when disciplined by technical limitations and editorial snaffles, as in the short story, this penchant really comes into its own. For if literature is the document of Life, the short story is the small print, the explication of which is essential reading for all who would seek the fullest possible understanding of the contract.

John Updike has observed that 'Irish ... literature gives us the impression of a race whose rich human nature has never been matched by its institutions or its climate.' Updike was being kind to leave it at that – but even after one has recorded the shortcomings (to put it no more provocatively) of Irish institutions, one is forced to acknowledge the benefits they have, however unwittingly, conferred. For the Irish writer they have been a necessary evil: they have repressed, but the grit of repression has produced many a pearl – even though repression, being consistently reinforced by suppression, usually resulted in the ejection of the oyster along with the pearl.

Of late, however, Ireland has been experiencing not exactly a wind of change, but at least a welcome breeze. Old moulds have not been broken but many have had a little lukewarm oil poured into them. And while the rest of the English-speaking world's literature, having been always the free and easy chronicler of surrounding contemporaneity, now finds itself blown into the shoals of boredom which produce mainly stultifying titillation and flatulent television drama, Ireland's new-found freedom to wriggle about in its straightjacket has enabled it to treat of themes which were up to recently taboo, to discuss deviations even the existence of which had hitherto not been recognized, and to express views and attitudes which only yesterday would have resulted in their propagator's ostracism or exile, or frequently both. This dispensation came at the psychologically perfect moment, when the Irish short story was entering the doldrums, for its maturity of technique meant that it was able to render the new material with that brand of under-stated revelation which constitutes the most powerful charge a short story can deliver; and it was set to produce this new wave of stories from that underworld which ever haunts the common man's unconscious at a time when a great number of story writers elsewhere had allowed themselves to be conned into writing about people and situations which had little relevance to real life, in prose which had little relevance to real literature. The result is that while in these places the short story has tended to reduce the size of its audience, in Ireland it has increased it.

If indeed contemporary Ireland is, for good or ill, drawing nearer to the open society one finds in most of the western world today, then one might fairly expect to see such a development reflected in any selection of stories culled from the best work of recent times. I don't think this anthology, which is composed of some unpublished stories and others which have appeared in periodicals during the past two years, should disappoint any such expectations. It suggests an Ireland in a state of flux, an Ireland of the old, but not ancient, and of the new, but not trendy. Traditional themes and traditional treatments are still lovingly engrossed, but one can also find recorded, alongside the stresses of a familiar culture being inexorably, if not rudely, reduced, the often traumatic responses of a hitherto shielded national sensibility forced at last to regard the unacceptable face of reality. And that all these tales are told not only with the individuality of touch and expression that has always been the hallmark of the Irish short story, but with the illuminating immediacy that is the short story's particular virtue, ensures their wide accessibility and appeal.

David Marcus

The Heel of the Hunt

JOHN A. RYAN

'Batty dear,' said Lady Catherine, 'you will have a little drink, won't you?'

He slipped an arm around her waist and ran with her up the steps. In the doorway he stopped and put a big hand on each of her hips and grinned at her. She noticed that he smelt pleasantly of horses.

'Tiddy, it's no wonder Sam is fond of you,' he said. 'You know exactly what a man needs.' He grinned again. 'Come in here behind the door with me —'

She escaped from him, laughing, a bit out of breath, and she was thinking not for the first time of the paradox that was Batty Harrington: a fine big man, any girl's fancy, and a charmer too when he liked, and yet the worst marriage risk in Ireland. She thought of Maggie then, and that made her sigh, not for Maggie of course but for Batty.

Her husband was placidly handing out drinks to the early-comers.

'A little something for Batty, Sam.'

Sam poured out a large Paddy and handed it across the table.

'I'm glad you came, Batty,' he said. 'I wanted to see you. Are you going to Punchestown?'

'Of course I'm going to Punchestown. I'll ask Bord Bainne to milk the cows.'

'That's all right,' said Sam. 'I'll send Peter Redmond over to do your cows, and the two young fellows can manage here. I suppose Wigeon will be able to come?'

'Is he not here?' asked Batty, and a little cloud that had been on the fringe of his consciousness grew just a little bigger and darker.

'No. Hasn't come yet,' Sam replied, and then, maybe realizing that Batty was disappointed, he added, 'Won't be much good to us today with that damaged wing, but he'll

13

surely put in an appearance later on.'

The meet at Coolgard House was notorious for being late in moving off. Sam Wilson loved hunting but he was incurably hospitable and this always delayed the start. It suited Batty, because Skoury wasn't able for a long day of it, not under Batty's weight. Today, however, things started early, probably due to the efforts of their new joint-master.

The day was cold, cloudy and dry. The wind was from the east. The horses' breath steamed as they moved down the drive. Well, a good hunting day, at any rate. Wigeon hadn't come, but with an arm in a sling, why should he? He'd probably be at Coolgard when they got back and then they could have a jar together. Batty sniffed that keen air and shivered, and it was not because of the cold, but the old primeval excitement and expectancy that never failed, never had failed in twenty years or more. He looked around and found Robin McCormick close behind him. 'Morrow, Robin. Good class of a day.'

''Tis a good day, Bat, however long 'twill last. 'Twill snow before night. And I don't like that one bit. Have you any hay you could sell me?'

'I'll tell you that on Patrick's Day,' and he looked at the grey sky and started mentally counting bales.

Out ahead, Tim Kelly was swearing fluently at his hounds, his blue-jowled head pushed well up into a bowler, while towards the rear of the hunt, sure enough, there was the new joint-master, Mrs Ruth Knatchbull, all the way from Pennsylvania. MFH. Mistress of Foxhounds. She was egging somebody on. She was an enthusiastic egger-on. What a face! What a moustache! Yoicks!

He began to think he shouldn't have had that last Paddy, but it was because he'd had to drink it off in a hurry. These Americans had no idea of the value of time. These cursagod ditches! They sound all right in lyrical things that you read in *Horse and Hound*. The Quorn. The misty morn and all that. The Quorn, the Quorn, the lusty Quorn. One of these days he'd be found dead in one of these gripes. A glorious death, but wet and uncomfortable.

They were taking the same route they had taken on that Stephen's Day, when was it? A year ago? Two? The day he

14

had grounded Sarah in Hearne's barn. Yoicks! He snorted with laughter. The horn, the horn, the lusty horn!

And there it was now, as Kelly blew his hounds out of the home covert, which in courtesy they had to draw but which wasn't worth wasting much time on.

He found old Canon Pettigrew beside him when they stopped near the Cashel road.

'They're slow in finding,' said the Canon. 'It's because of all the rain.'

Batty tried to recall when they'd had all the rain, but as well as he could remember it hadn't rained for a fortnight.

'You'll catch a cold, Canon. What happened to your hat?'

'I'm afraid it must have fallen off,' he said, peering around uncertainly.

Good job his head is screwed on, thought Batty. It was never easy to know just how conscious the Canon was.

Hounds were working at a high place of briars and rusty bracken. Nolan's *lios*. They'd get nothing there only fairies. Tim Kelly must have been thinking the same way. He shook up his hounds and took them smartly away, moving north towards the higher ground. After drawing a blank at Jacobs', they tried Hogan's knock, and at once got results. A loud blast on the huntsman's horn was answered by the music of the hounds. Rounding a corner, Batty nearly ran into the Canon, who was standing in his stirrups, staring in the opposite direction to that taken by the pack and shouting at the top of his voice, 'Gone away!' It's his brains, thought Batty, and laughed, and shouted, 'This way, Canon!'

He took the longer way round Burke's to avoid the stony lane and he remembered another day when Wigeon, after being similarly hindered by the Canon, had come up to them, red-faced, spluttering, 'That blunderin' old eejit, Canon Pettigrew, got right across me, nearly had me off. Silly old bugger, always gettin' in the way, with his owl's head on him, and that stupid-lookin' animal of his like a cross between a jackass and a ... a ...'

'Come, Mr Stewart,' Lady Catherine had interposed. 'You have a wonderful flow of language but you do know that poor Canon Pettigrew doesn't see very well.'

'He's well able to see what I put on the plate of a Sunday,'

Wigeon had said, winking at Batty. Wigeon's rages produced more fun than fury and never lasted long.

The gallop came to a stop beyond Burke's when they lost their fox at the little stream that runs down into Minaun. They climbed the farther slope and reached the level again through an open gate. He mopped his face with a large white handkerchief and then carefully wiped Skoury's neck and tickled him behind his ear and whispered to him as they moved slowly across a ploughed field.

Now who was that on Robin's gelding? A likely-looking bit. It must be one of Robin's daughters, but they couldn't be that age yet. What a thigh! He raised his cap very civilly.

'Some idiot drove his sheep right across the line in front of us,' she snarled. It was one of Robin's daughters all right. She sounded just like the gentle Pauline.

'Some of these country fellows haven't a clue,' he said mildly.

'Peasants!' she hissed. She had a luscious mouth, for all that. Like her mother, Pauline Kerr.

Peasants they used to be, now they're all gentlemen; Robin no less, himself no less, and this strapping wench with the pouting red lips a peasant's daughter, God bless her. Fine girl you are, steer clear or Robin might want him to marry her. What she didn't know — how could she? — was that the peasant with the sheep was young Dave Burke whose father, Dave, had grounded Pauline in the old days. That, of course, was before Pauline sobered up and married Robin.

Whoa, there, Skoury! Must let out that iron a bit, his left leg was hurting again, memento of Killatiarna, by God that was a day and a half. He swung to the ground and then remembered his flask.

'Batty, is something the matter?' It was Lady Catherine. Me fly is open, he said, but not out loud, you didn't say things like that to Lady Catherine. He went to slip the flask back into his pocket, and then thought, Hell! Why?

'Would you like a little drop to warm you?'

'Why, thank you, Batty.' She was a good sport. She didn't really want it and he suspected that though she put the flask to her mouth she drank none. What a woman she must have been in her day. She still had two of the finest legs in the

16

county.

But as they waited together near the Lacken covert, he was thinking of another similar encounter, not with Lady Catherine but with Maggie.

'Have a jorum, Maggie. 'Twill tighten the elastic in your knickers.'

'You're deplorably vulgar, Batty,' she had said, coming up close beside him and digging her knee into him.

'I know, I know. It's the way I'm made. But I'm irresistible to women,' and he had looked down at her, grinning.

'Are you sure you mean irresistible? Are you sure you don't mean irresponsible?'

That wasn't his line of country at all, so he had only grunted and said, 'Don't drink all that.'

He remembered, however, the way she had persisted. 'You really do believe that. You really believe you're the answer to any maiden's prayer. And that's the rock you'll perish on, Batty.'

She had said it in such a way that from that day on he had been a bit scared of her and had never felt as free and easy with her as before.

It was the hounds giving tongue in a very businesslike way that jerked him from his reverie.

'They've put up something,' said Lady Catherine, and sure enough when they rounded the covert, there was the pack stretching out up a half-ploughed stubble. Batty yelled 'He'll have to give us a run. He's headed away from the hill,' and at that moment he caught a glimpse of the fox on the wintry horizon just before he disappeared. They swept on and were soon labouring up that same stubble. He could feel the lift and thrust of Skoury's shoulders as he leaned forward, and then he gave him a breather as they stepped up a stony lane towards the top, joined now by several other riders. Then out again into the open, and a glorious run began, right the full length of Benire valley, Lady Catherine thundering along beside him, away out in front hounds at full stretch. Kelly struggling to keep in touch, he could see no one else, the wind cold and cutting on his face. There really was nothing in the whole world to compare with it after all.

Their fox took them straight across the muddy place at the

17

bottom of Jefferies' fields. The pack managed it with difficulty, but of course it wouldn't hold a horse.

'Keep up,' he yelled at Lady Catherine. 'The gap is in a wicked state. You'd go to the elder in it,' and they kept along the higher level and jumped the stream farther on. Glancing back he saw that at least three of the others were stuck at the muddy place and he laughed loud. 'The old dog,' he shouted. But Lady Catherine was now losing ground and he was on his own. Not quite. Two others were off to the right — one of them was surely that English fellow, the other looked like Tom Loughlin — but they seemed to have come across by Barnakillen lane and hadn't come over the hill at all.

He and Tim Kelly had it all to themselves and at the end of that great run, one of the best he thought that they'd ever had, he was still there when they killed, right under Bawncreea wall.

Very small their brave fox looked now, that had been so full of running and of guile so short a time before. He had been beaten by less than two hundred yards for the break in the wall and the safety of Bawncreea wood.

Tim and Batty shook hands solemnly. Respect for hard riders and contempt for lesser men was in that handshake. Then Tim took his tired hounds away towards Bawncreea cross. The light was beginning to fail. Batty headed for Coolgard, hacking first along the level, but then walking where he met the long rise to the main road.

Now on the long trudge back, he felt elation draining out of him. Why he should think of Maggie again he didn't know. She should be here. Instead she was likely out with the Kildares or whoever hunted up in that part of the country. Who would have thought she was all that interested in getting married? And that bit of a fellow, a lightweight, hardly any taller than Maggie herself, he'd never be able for her. 'Capable of producing hunters,' the phrase jumped, oddly, to his mind. If any woman was calculated to produce high-quality stock, surely it was Maggie. But whoever was getting hunters on Maggie now, it wasn't Batty.

He shook his head as if to shake away the idea. Well, there were others. There was that viperish young filly with the pouty mouth, Pauline Kerr's daughter. Too young! Too young for you! Now what put that thought in his head? He was only forty-three, going on — what? Next week? — well, not forty-four yet. But she's only eighteen or nineteen. Oh hell, if they're big enough they're old enough.

There was a light already in Flanagan's, one of the famous oil lamps; with windows a foot square their lighting-up time was bound to be early. Anything except temptation, he thought, and going round to the back he left Skoury in the stable. 'Five minutes, Skoury,' he said.

He took his drink over to the fire and sat down in the welcome warmth. At the other side sat a small man drinking a large stout. That was Tom Callaghan, spoiled poteen-maker, grave-digger and handy man.

'Good morrow, Tom.'

Tom looked up slowly and surveyed him from heel to head.

'Jaysus,' he said. 'Comfort me in me last agony,' and went back to his stout.

Not an easy man to talk to, reflected Batty.

After long silence, Tom asked, with heavy sarcasm, 'Well, did yiz ketch anything?'

'What have you against the hunt crowd Tom?'

'Idlers. Idlers and their fancy women. Tell the truth of you, though, Batty, you were never an idler.'

'And no fancy women either,' said Batty, and then was sorry he'd said it. 'Did you ever hunt, Tom?'

'Oh ay. Isn't that what killed all belongin' to me?'

'It's a thing that grows on you. If you once follow hounds on a good horse, you'll never again ask for any other sport.'

'I must saddle the jennet,' said Tom sourly.

Uncheered by his stop at Flanagan's, he set off on the last half mile. Near Fitzgerald's he saw a hound that looked very like a straggler from the pack. It wasn't like Tim to lose one of them. Batty whistled him, but the animal loped away.

As Coolgard House came in view he was reminded of the last time they'd had the Hunt Ball there. A night and a half! A night till morning! He remembered sitting on the broad carpeted stairway with Wigeon beside him, glasses of malt in their hands, studying the legs of the women who went up and down the stairs, and exchanging pleasantries with them all. Wigeon wasn't long back home after a trip to England with some beef group and he spoke as though he had managed to escape from something he never wanted to see again.

'We don't know how well off we are in this country. Do you know what? The first time I asked for a drink over there they had to search the house to find a bottle of whiskey. They had Scotch of course, but I'm talking about real whiskey. And when they found it the girl in the bar poured out a little drop and 'clare to God it hardly wet the bottom of the glass.' He looked mournfully at Batty. 'Do you remember when we were goin' to school they told us an atom was the smallest thing that could hould be itself? Well, that's not true. The smallest thing in the world is the English measure of whiskey.'

'I'd believe you,' said Batty, but he wasn't giving all his attention to the conversation because he could see Maggie almost directly below him and with that low-cut dress she was wearing he could look down between Galteemore and Slievanamon. She looked up and saw him and made a puss at him, and at once he stood up and went down to her, ignoring Wigeon's 'What ails you?' and leaving his whiskey on the stairs, because whiskey can be replaced but opportunity can't.

He shook his head again. That was all water under the bridge now.

At Coolgard House he said 'I'll put you in your box, Skoury.' He gave him a quick rub-down, fastened a blanket on him and left him munching in his box. He would just have a quick look to see if Wigeon had come, then he must get on home.

Going up the steps, he felt the tiredness and a twinge of pain in his hurt leg. He stopped for a moment and looked across the trees at the lowering sky, and a snowflake drifted down and landed on his sleeve. Must get home, he thought. He went into the hall, which was pleasantly warm after the raw air outside. A pert and plump girl wearing a little white cap and a little white apron was crossing the hall with a tray.

'Kitty, is Willie Stewart here?' he asked her.

'No sir.'

He hadn't really expected him, yet he felt keenly disappointed. It wasn't his way to show it however.

'Begod, Kitty, you're puttin' on weight. It looks well on you, though,' and he made a rawm at her.

'Stop, Batty. I mean sir. You'll make me drop all the glasses.'

He was standing near the garden window and he could see the sullen clouds darkening outside. He found himself wishing that he hadn't to go home; here there were lights and warmth and people. For a while he stood watching the flakes of snow that fell against the glass and melted, and his thoughts were bleak.

Well, there was work waiting to be done, animals to be fed and seen to, and these things wouldn't wait. He turned heavily towards the door. But now Sam had seen him and came over.

'Batty, I didn't see you come in. What will you have? I know you can't stay, but have some little thing before you go.'

Batty hesitated. Then he said 'I'll have a drop of Rémy Martin,' but it wasn't because he wanted it. Nor was it camaraderie that made him say it. It was, rather, a kind of terror. It was something very like defeat.

Out of Great Tribulation Cometh Truth

PATRICK BOYLE

In the soft sand beneath the cliffs, they sat around in their swimming togs watching him — McGill, idly scratching at his matted chest, Clancy and Byrne, hairless teenagers, hugging their shins as they rocked back and forth in time with the gyrations of the tall muscular figure intent on his pre-swim loosening-up exercises.

'You should be in powerful form for the match tomorrow, Mick, judging by your antics,' jeered McGill.

Regan straightened up with a grunt, clutched his head and released a loud groan that tailed off into a massive yawn.

'It'll be the grace of God if I don't fall asleep in the water,' he said.

Clancy gave a little cluck of commiseration.

'A late night?' he suggested hesitantly.

'Or a gut-full of beer?' said Byrne.

'More likely a hen-bird?' said McGill.

Regan hawked far back in his throat and vented a dry spit.

'All three,' he said.

With the back of his hand he rubbed his lips.

'To say nothing but the truth, I'm shagged out. Drinking beyond in the hotel for half the night. And then till morning stretched out above on the cliff head. Hammering a job.'

He laughed ruefully.

'At the latter end, the pair of us fell asleep.'

With wagging forefinger and mock-serious face, he admonished them, 'There's one important discovery I made, lads. You have little stomach for nookey when you wake up beside your dame at six o'clock on a windy morning. And you wringing wet with dew.'

Clancy was gazing at him, a look of concern on his face.

'But won't that affect your game tomorrow?' he said.

'Breaking training and all that.'

'Who was the bird?' said McGill.

Regan frowned.

'It will be a poor day for football in this country if the game is taken over by a crowd of craw-thumpers.'

He paused and his face relaxed.

'One of the Drohans of the Terrace, Jim,' he said.

'Which of them was it?' McGill asked.

'The young one. Agnes.'

'Oh, a useful article.'

Byrne, who was following the conversation with the beady-eyed impatience of a hungry robin, cut in: 'You're dead right, Jim. She's dying for it. But I can tell you one thing for sure.'

He paused dramatically. Then went on in a low, earnest voice. 'The last time out, I took the hunger off her.'

'The hard man himself,' murmured McGill.

He raised his eyes to heaven and carolled softly,

Anyone you can screw, he can screw better.

'Begod,' said Regan, 'the few months at the university seem to have filled out the fork of his trousers. Maybe when Clancy goes there it will soften his cough.'

Clancy, very red in the face, struggled for words.

'You-you-you've got me wrong, Mick. It's just that I thought . . . all that beer, you know . . . you'd have trouble getting your second wind.'

'Balls!' said Regan. 'The few jars never harmed anyone. On the field or off.'

'You can say that again,' said Byrne. 'The last match I played, I was footless drunk going on the pitch. And I never played a better game.'

McGill shook his head sadly. He intoned: 'Where none admire, 'tis useless to excel. Words taken, my dear brethren, from the label of an empty beer bottle.'

'Stow it, Jim,' said Regan. 'You'll draw down the drouth on me.'

He turned to survey the beach.

'What's brought all the crowd here today?' he said.

The strand was dotted with groups of people, paddling sedately in the shallow water. Shirt-sleeved men with trousers rolled knee-high and women in sombre shapeless clothes, their skirts hoisted a discreet few inches above the surface of the tide.

'Oh, they're the Salt-waters,' said McGill. 'That's what they're known as locally. They're mountainy ones who come here for a holiday every year around this time.'

'They're queer looking ducks,' said Regan.

'You could hardly call them that,' said McGill. 'It has never been known for one of them to take to the water.'

'Though,' he added, 'they *do* waddle about on the fringe of the tide.'

'Sure the poor devils,' Clancy's tone was apologetic, 'I suppose none of them can swim a stroke. Living so far away from the sea.'

'Aren't you from Roscrea?' said Byrne. 'And wasn't Mick here,' he pointed at Regan, 'born and bred in the Midlands? And yet he has a roomful of swimming trophies.'

McGill grinned sardonically.

'At that rate, a young fellow like you, living here beside the sea, should be a bloody Channel swimmer. Instead of splashing around trying to keep yourself afloat.'

'I can swim as well as the next one.'

'That's what *you* think.'

Regan cut in: 'Come on, you lazy hoors, or the tide'll be on the turn.'

They scrambled to their feet and followed him down the beach, Clancy and Byrne ranging themselves on either side of the tall, swaggering figure. Slouching in the rear, McGill eyed them sardonically — Clancy, almost as tall as Regan but still soft with puppy fat, listening with grave attention to what Regan was saying; Byrne, small and skinny, nodding his head vigorously in agreement. Two disciples, McGill decided, linked by their devotion to the Master.

On the edge of the beach, loud with the roar of the surf, they stooped and, dipping casual fingers in the bubbling foam, went through the motions of blessing themselves.

'There's a heavy ground swell,' said Regan. 'Must have been a storm somewhere yesterday.'

He watched his feet sink into the sand with the suction of the receding wave.

'Tide's going out too. You'd want to watch for undertow.'

24

'Do you hear that, Byrne?' said Clancy. 'Better not go out too far.'

'Stop worrying, will you! Sure if you keep swimming on the surface of the water, how can undertow affect you?'

'A nice point,' said McGill. 'But I wouldn't stress it too much, if I were you.'

'Keep in your own depth anyway,' Clancy persisted.

'But don't I tell you —'

Regan burst out impatiently, 'Stop nattering, you silly bastards.'

He broke away from them and charged into the surf, diving into the maw of a breaker. Clancy and Byrne plunged after him, Byrne staggering to his feet in the shallow trough of the wave only to be engulfed by the succeeding one.

McGill laughed.

'It's the price of you,' he muttered.

He waded cautiously in, breasting the smaller waves, backing against the steeper ones, paying no heed to the jeering of his friends. At length he allowed a roller to lift him, legs and arms sprawling, until in its wake he settled himself back in the water to float, keeping himself sidelong to the waves so that they rocked him gently as they passed underneath. Isolated by the rumble of surf and the muffled wailing of the gulls, he squinted up at the sun and, through his scorched eyelids, felt it soak up all semblance of coherent thought. Incuriously he noted the cloud of spray shrouding the beach, the litter of uprooted seaweed floating around him, the sand-choked surface of the waves. He caught glimpses of the other three swimming around with dedicated energy — Regan and Clancy, whipping up trails of foam in a vigorous crawl; Byrne, labouring along with a clumsy floundering breast stroke. All urging themselves onward. With kicking legs and flailing arms. As though the sea were something to be mastered. A plunging dangerous animal to be subdued only by force.

Stupid poor sods, decided McGill. Always trying to prove themselves. Worried that someone else might run or jump or swim better than they can. God give them wit. He eased back his head and allowed himself to relax into the kindly element that sustained him. The water lapped and gurgled in his ears, salted pleasantly his lips and swung his limp body back and forth like a frond of seaweed swaying in the tide. Overhead a solitary gull coasted, its outstretched wings tilting from side to side as though balancing itself on an invisible tightrope. With beady eye it scoured the sea and through the clamour of the waves its screeching call came faintly to his ears.

'Kwaaay! Kwaaay!'

There was something oddly urgent in the high-pitched throaty cry. As though the bird were trying to attract attention. Lifting his head clear of the water, he studied the flight of the soaring, swooping gull.

Once more the cry came. From right behind him.

'Hey! Hey!'

He rolled over, facing towards the sound.

It was Byrne who was kicking up the commotion. Chest-deep in the water, he appeared, judging from the rapid movements of his body, to be giving an impersonation of someone running against the motion of an endless belt. For a few seconds he would keep up this corny routine and then fall forward in a flurry of waving arms into the water, only to stagger up again, coughing and spluttering and shouting as he resumed his childish antics.

McGill snorted. Proper little notice-box. Acting the canister, as usual. Must be the leading man in every show. Got to be slapped down continually. Or he'd be a right bloody nuisance. Still there's nothing wrong with the poor devil that a good kick on the arse wouldn't cure.

He was about to shout a jeering comment when he noticed that Byrne, who had collapsed once more into the water, was now trying to keep himself afloat with a frantic attempt at a breast stroke. He kept slewing around in all directions, his poked-up head turning this way and that like a rat drowning in a barrel. In a high squeaky voice he kept up a gasping litany of cries.

'Help! Help!'

McGill was shocked. This was surely a bit much. The bloody little shaper. Trying to cod the troops with such a phoney act. Doesn't he know that mocking is catching. It would be the price of him if —

And with that everything clicked into place. The summer Byrne was learning to swim. A hopeless job. His arms and

26

legs going through the motions. But the timing all wrong. Quick and jerky like a clockwork toy. Only he never gained an inch. Just kept gradually sinking. Down and down till he reached the bottom. Stirring up the sand so that it swirled around him. Still trying to keep afloat. Like he is now. With that jerky clockwork breast stroke.

'Jesus, he's maybe in trouble,' McGill muttered.

Before he could move, Clancy had swum the few strokes across, shouting, 'Are you all right, Kevin?'

He stood up, to comfort or curse mattered not, for he at once tumbled back as though a rug had been pulled from under his feet. He stumbled to his feet, only to go down again. The third time, he staggered to his feet with Byrne hanging onto his back like a limpet, arms round his neck, legs round his waist, shouting for help as Clancy strove to shake him off.

With the feeling that something very odd was happening, McGill sought bottom and tried to stand upright. But though he was only chest-deep, he could get no foothold. Instead of a firm bottom, the sand was sweeping past at such a speed that it was impossible to achieve purchase. As he splashed around trying to keep his feet, he was alarmed to notice that they had all drifted down the strand until now they were quite close to the rocks. With the current now sweeping around and taking them out to sea. A particularly urgent cry from Byrne decided him. It was every man for himself from now on. And the sooner he got started, the better.

Regan appeared to have come to the same conclusion, for he was already making for the shore. Not with his usual immaculate textbook crawl but with a frantic effort of flailing arms and feet.

'Hey, Buster!' McGill shouted.

Regan did not answer. Nor did he slacken speed. Just for a second his head slewed round to draw breath and his evasive eyes met those of McGill with a curious glance of distaste.

McGill was dismayed. He's pulling out all right, he decided, as he started after Regan. And if a swimmer of his calibre reckons it's time to quit, who can blame the rest of us for making tracks? He must have figured out that this bloody current is too powerful to play around with. But that look on his ugly puss was an eye-opener. An unmistakable warning to shag off. Oh, it's every man for himself, all right.

Threshing his way through the water in a clumsy attempt at a crawl, McGill found himself falling further and further behind until at length he was forced to fall back on his normal routine — a steady plodding breast stroke. Doggedly he strove to propel himself forward with the growing realization that he was barely holding his own. That soon he would be losing ground. That if he slackened at all, he would undoubtedly be sucked out to sea.

By this time, Regan had reached the shore and was wading through the shallows without a backward glance. Curse of God on him, raged McGill. Friendship means nothing to the heartless bowzie. But bejesus, he'll not get away with this piece of treachery. He'll be shown up as the gutless bastard that he is.

At the edge of the tide, the Salt-waters paddled or sat about in the sun. Children built sand castles or gathered shells or poked about in rock pools for crabs. Far up on the strand, a black and white collie raced frantically after the shadow of a seagull.

McGill felt in some way aggrieved at this display of normality. There should have been some sign of excitement. Groups gathered together pointing seawards. Women wringing their hands. Men shouting encouragement through cupped hands. Instead of having to fight for life not a stone's throw from a mob of unheeding country folk. He watched Regan thread his way heedlessly through the crowd, his insolent swagger that of an acclaimed hero. On the cliff top, two black-robed nuns gazed ahead, armoured in indifference. Nothing could be heard through the continuous rumble of the surf. And yet the beach must be alive with the noise of children — chattering voices and gay laughter and shrill cries of protest. It was unthinkable that his own cries of protest, were he driven to utter them, would be swallowed up in the roar of the sea.

He chanced a quick glance back to see how Clancy was making out. Still struggling with his unwelcome burden, he was floundering around, wrenching at the skinny arms clamped tenaciously about his throat. He appeared to be making no progress whatever towards the shore.

Dismayed, McGill buried his head in the water, urging himself forward, arms and legs working like pistons, in an effort to gain ground. Beneath him he could see sand and shingle and seaweed rushing past. But he knew with sickening certainty that this was no indication of his progress, just a reminder of the speed of the undertow. The resistance seemed to have gone out of the water. No grip to it. As though you were hung up in harness and swimming in air. At last, lungs bursting and muscles worked out, he eased off, only to find, when he gazed round him, that he was no longer holding his ground.

Giving up hope of mastering the current, he abandoned all effort to keep afloat. Instead he attempted to wade ashore. It was no use. Again and again he sought a foothold, pedalling madly to achieve a grip in the shifting sand, only to finish up sprawling his length in the sea.

He tried to get a grip on himself. Take it easy, he urged. Or you'll finish up as Byrne did. A windy bastard squealing for help. Much good it would do you anyway. In this inferno. And even if you were heard shouting, who's to help you? Not one of the mountainy yobs, that's for sure. None of them can swim a stroke. And Clancy is otherwise engaged. As for Regan. Look at him! Slippy-tit in person. Standing straddle-legged beneath the cliffs. Drying his dirty carcase. With his backside turned to the congregation. Not for the sake of modesty. Oh, no! Just so that he'll witness nothing of what's happening out here at sea. A bloody walking Judas.

McGill tried to control his whirling thoughts. No use now trying to swim to the beach. A waste of energy. The only course left is to face out to sea. Go with the current. And try to escape out of it obliquely. Before it rounds the rocky peninsula skirting the bay.

Lest he should have second thoughts, he swung round at once and headed out for the open sea. He struck out for the last cluster of rocks, shaggy and half submerged, at the very tip of the narrow out-thrust ridge. Surely this would be his best chance to edge his way out of the current and clamber to safety.

29

As he surveyed the terrifying expanse of empty ocean, he was overwhelmed by a sensation of utter loneliness. Even the familiar rumble of the surf was muted. Instead there was a continuous sizzling gurgle as though the water through which he moved had been brought to the boil or was exposed to a torrential downpour of rain. The surface of the sea writhed and pulsed and simmered as the current fought to subdue the waves. Ahead of him, a wide track had been driven through the lines of breakers, breakers that had ploughed their way unbroken across the Atlantic. This manifestation of furious energy rendered McGill's isolation more daunting. For how could he hope to escape a force against which the waves themselves were defenceless.

Tiring rapidly and beginning to despair, he was ready to give up the struggle when once more he heard a gull scream. A long-drawn-out wail, the echo of his own unuttered cry. Desolate though the cry sounded, it brought a small measure of comfort to McGill. At least he was not alone in his loneliness.

Again the gull screamed. And screaming, swooped. To hover expectantly, dangling feet almost brushing the sea. For a brief moment it fluttered, neck outstretched and yellow beak hungrily probing. Then it settled on the scummy water a few yards ahead, tucking its wings primly into place.

To McGill, the grey and white bird was a symbol of hope. He was convinced that it had alighted near him because it too was lonely and abandoned. Whilst they bore each other company – bird and man – neither would come to harm. And so he struggled on, his gaze continually drawn away from the weed-covered rocks at the end of the reef, the target of his choice, to the solitary gull floating on the water so close to him.

He could distinguish the flight feathers of the wings, a black and white cluster, cocked up jauntily over the neatly folded tail. And the sleek white head moving constantly from side to side as it eyed the horizon or ducked down to peck at its breast feathers.

From the Island it must have come. Colonies of sea birds nest there. Thousands of them. Flying in to the mainland every morning. Screeching with the hunger. And back again at evening gorged with food. Sailing across the sky. Not a sound out of them. Flying in wedge formation. All the groups converging on the one path. Out across the glittering sea. To where the sun is sinking behind the Island.

McGill scanned the empty horizon. Somewhere beyond the tumbling breakers was the Island. A low-lying rocky mass. Elusive as the Isles of the Blest. For on spring tides, nothing could be seen of it from the mainland. Except the hulk of a wrecked ship. Perched on the skyline. As though in dry dock. Always he had promised himself that some day, somehow, he would get out to the Island. Maybe bring gear and stay the night. Alone. For no one from the mainland goes there anymore. Not since the wreck was sacked and plundered years ago.

But now he might never set foot on the Island. Never get the chance to fall asleep encompassed by the sound of breakers. Or to wake up in the morning with no other company than a skyful of birds. Overwhelmed with self-pity, he groaned aloud.

The gull craned round and gazed at him. Yellow-rimmed eyes unblinking. Containing only a message of pitiless indifference. The bird was now so close to him that, swimming with his eyes almost at water level, he was forced to look up at it — a monstrous creature, balanced so lightly on a wave crest that its body could have been inflated by air. It made him conscious of his own clumsy body, kept afloat only by the exertion of his tired limbs.

Suddenly he remembered how, as a kid camping out, he had woken up one morning on his ground-sheet to discover, towering over him, a squatting rabbit that gazed down at him with grave impassive eyes. This encounter had shocked him profoundly. For the few seconds it lasted, he was faced with the possibility that all the doctrines and beliefs he had accepted without question were delusions. That compared with this magnificent bronze colossus, he was still the puny cowering product of the last day of creation.

McGill scowled at the heedless bird.

'You can be done without. You and the like of you,' he muttered.

The bird did not move.

With the palm of his hand, McGill beat the water petulantly.

'Shag off!' he hissed. 'D'you hear me?'

'Kek-kek-kek-kek-kek!' The gull rose, cackling with crazy laughter.

McGill glared up at the wheeling bird.

'You jeering hoor!' he shouted. 'You're as bad as the rest of them.

He slewed round and struck out for the nearest stretch of rock, feeling the current drag at him again as he turned sideways on to it. But now, instead of flogging weary muscles into action, his flailing arms and threshing legs, stiffened by defiance, drove him steadily forward. They're all the bloody same, he raged, as he buried his head in the water and battled on. Waiting for you to shout for help. Or pray for salvation. Or whimper as your past life is unfolded. In all its welter of sin.

Above the roar in his ears of pounding blood, he heard once more the shrill cackling of the gull. For an instant he jerked his head back, glimpsing an empty sky, a stretch of gaunt dripping rock and an expanse of treacherous sea.

'No matter,' he muttered. 'I'll make it in spite of them all.'

He lowered his head once more and forced himself onwards. It was really not so far to the rocks, he consoled himself. Maybe half the length of a football pitch. In a muddled way, he tried to figure out how many trudgen strokes would be needed to cover the distance. Fifty? A hundred? God knows how many, when you allow for the pull of the current. Better tackle it in spurts. Ten strokes and a breather. A chance to see what ground you've made. But the urge to lift his head after the first few strokes became ever more pressing. Just a glimpse, he pleaded. A quick glance. To see what ground has still to be covered. And each time he looked, the rocks seemed as far away as ever. Worse still, the current was pulling him farther and farther out towards the open sea.

Panic gripped him. Eyes squeezed shut, he thrust himself through the water, arms and legs moving frantically in a last effort to reach the rocks before the current whipped him out beyond the reef. He urged himself on, still counting the rapid movements of his weary arms.

When the first tendril of sea thong brushed across his face, he did not break off the count. Sixty-four. Sixty-five. Sixty-six. Even when a clammy tongue of seaweed licked his shoulder, he kept struggling on. Seventy-two. Seventy-three. Seventy-four. Only when he found himself entangled in a dense mass of seaweed, did he tread water and peer about him.

He was still some distance from the rocks, but the stretch of water intervening was brown with seaweed. The surface of the sea was alive with swaying fronds; the breakers shaggy with matted wrack. For a moment he was caught up in the childhood fantasy that these terrifying fronds and tentacles would clutch at his arms, his legs, his body, and draw him down to his death on the sea-bed.

And then the realization burst upon him that here indeed was his deliverance. That though he was too exhausted by now to contend with the current, he could still pull himself ashore by means of the rooted seaweed. The long fronds and fibres, caught in the undertow, streamed out like anchor ropes. Grasping cluster after cluster of seaweed, he began to haul himself along towards the rocks. Sometimes fronds would become uprooted or slither from his grip. It mattered not. There was such a profusion of seaweed that even a random grab could not fail to connect with a fresh cluster. Now and again he was overcome with revulsion as the clammy tendrils coiled round his body. He would flounder around in the midst of the sea wrack, legs and arms flapping convulsively, getting himself more and more entangled, until at length, gasping and spluttering, he would once more start hauling himself to safety with the aid of the very substance he so loathed and feared.

By the time he reached the reef, he was so exhausted that it was only with the greatest difficulty that he managed to clamber up on the slimy rocks. Cautiously he worked his way across the wave-swept ridge, crawling mostly on hands and knees, where but a short while before he would have leapt from spur to spur. So shaken was he that even when he had reached the high rocks above tide level, he remained crouched on all fours, too terrified to straighten up. When at last he scrambled to his feet, it was to find that all about him was the world of normality. Out to sea, the waves trooped in to shore — portly, dignified, dependable — like suburban commuters hurrying to their bus stops. Below on the beach, the mountainy folk continued to sit in the sun. To paddle in the tide. To walk the strand with bare feet and rolled-up pants. The sheep dog, balked of shadows to chase, crouched at the water's edge, barking at the crumbling waves. The two nuns on the cliff top stood gazing down at the crowded beach. It was impossible to credit that anything untoward could have happened in this setting.

And then, from the foot of the rocks, he heard a cry.

'Don't! Oh, don't!'

Crossing carefully to the edge of the reef, he looked down. Clancy, with Byrne still clinging to his back, was wading ankle-deep through the shallow water beyond reach of the waves. As he trudged on, bowed beneath the load, he sought to detach the human limpet by tearing at the clutching arms and legs. A group of children, gathered on the fringe of the tide, watched with interest these grown-up capers. Embarrassed by their scrutiny, Clancy made a final attempt to rid himself of the incubus.

'Let go of me, you idiot,' he hissed, shaking himself like a dog just in from the rain.

With a squeal of terror, Byrne released his grip and went sprawling in the water. He scrambled to his feet immediately, but remained rooted to the spot, gazing imploringly after the retreating figure of Clancy.

'Help!' he called. 'Help!'

The children took up the cry.

'Help! Help! Help!' they screamed, dancing with glee. Byrne paid no heed.

'Clancy!' he screamed, shaking his fist threateningly. 'Come back, Clancy!'

Now thoroughly aroused, the children rushed into the water, waving their arms in the air.

'Come back, Clancy!' they jeered. 'Come back, Clancy!'

A sandy-haired youngster, darting forward a few paces, began to chant, in time with his jerking knees and flapping hands:

34

*'Clan ... cy ... Clan ... cy ... Come ... back ... Clan
... cy.'*

The rest of the children joined in the chorus, prancing
about in the shallow water, their knees lifted high, raising
a curtain of spray from their stamping feet.

*'Clan ... cy ... Clan ... cy ... Come ... back ... Clan
... cy.'*

From his vantage point on the rocks, McGill watched the
scene in disgust.

'Jesus Christ!' he muttered through clenched teeth.

Clancy had come to a halt a few yards up the beach and
stood, back turned to the sea, shifting his feet uneasily in the
sand. At length, embarrassed by the jeering chorus invoking
his aid, he turned and retraced his steps.

The children fell silent as he approached, but remained
clustered together, eyeing him warily. He did not speak until
he reached the helpless figure.

'Come on,' he said. 'You're out of danger now.'

Byrne did not move. He gazed at Clancy, petrified.

'Snap out of it, man,' said Clancy. 'Don't be acting the
lug.'

He made to turn away.

'Don't go,' Byrne pleaded. 'Don't leave me. Please.'

Clancy gripped the outstretched hand and led him
forward, Byrne shuffling along with exaggerated caution as
though they were traversing a quagmire.

McGill waited till they reached dry land, then clambered
down from the rocks and joined them. No greetings were
exchanged and no one spoke as they walked slowly back up
the beach, followed for part of the way by the children.

Regan, by now fully dressed, was squatting on the sand,
tying his shoelaces. He looked up as they drew near.

'Well, if it isn't the three water sprites,' he said. 'I thought
you were never coming out.'

Stiffly he pushed himself to his feet, stamped his right foot
a few times into the soft sand and, stooping, commenced to
knead the thigh muscles.

'Got a muscle-lock when I was swimming,' he said, without
raising his head. 'Bloody dangerous thing. Had to chuck in
the sponge and come ashore.'

35

There was a low murmur of sympathy.

'Well, I'll be off now, lads,' he said, gathering up his swimming trunks and towel. 'Must punch in a bit of practice for the match tomorrow.'

As he swaggered off, they called after him, 'See you after the game.'

'We'll be rooting for you, Mick.'

'Good luck.'

In silence, they started to towel themselves, turned studiously away from each other, grunting and puffing self-consciously as they went through the pretence of drying their already sun-dried bodies. They avoided each other's gaze as, silently, they faced away from the strand to strip off their bathing togs, groping beneath modestly draped towels. Clad in shirts and trousers, they sat on the beach, staring out to sea whilst the silence became more and more unbearable. At length, McGill cleared his throat.

'It's a wonder he didn't say something,' he reflected.

Clancy picked up a handful of sand and watched it trickle out through his fist.

'Who?' he asked.

'Regan, of course, you dumb-cluck,' said McGill. 'Why didn't he say something?'

'Say something?' Clancy repeated.

'Yes. Any shagging thing at all. Instead of walking off without a word to throw to a dog.'

Clancy picked up another fistful of sand.

'But he did. Didn't he say he had to do a spell of training for the match tomorrow?'

'That doesn't explain away very much, does it?'

'Well, if you get a muscle-lock when you're in swimming, it would be as well for you to get loosened up before an important match the next day.'

'He must be in poor enough condition when he gets muscle-locked so easily.'

'You can get a muscle-lock lying in bed. If you give a sudden twist. It's happened to me often.'

McGill gave a scoffing laugh.

'Muscle-lock, how are you! You should have seen him making for the shore like a shot off a shovel.'

36

He stooped to examine closely the big toe of his right foot, stroking its contours lovingly.

'You would know at once,' he said, 'that there was a sinking ship around.'

Clancy glanced at him, a shocked expression on his face.

'That's not a nice thing to say,' he protested.

'I don't know how else you could describe it.'

Slowly Clancy rubbed the sand from the palms of his hands.

'Well, if that is the case,' he said, choosing his words carefully, 'there were more rats than one making for the shore.'

McGill glowered at him.

'You can speak for yourself,' he said. 'For I had to swim out to sea. Not in to shore. It was the luck of God I made dry land at all.'

Clancy leaned across and gripped McGill by the knee.

'At least, Jim —' He glanced quickly over his shoulder at Byrne, who was lying back on the sand, arms outstretched, eyes closed, breathing softly through parted lips. 'At least you hadn't the sinking ship moored to your back, the way I had.'

McGill pushed away the mollifying hand.

'You were doing your best to get rid of the load,' he said.

'No wonder,' said Clancy. 'I was nearly strangled.'

Grabbing up his socks, McGill pulled them on, twisting them this way and that as the heels persisted in buckling up around his insteps. A laundry label, stapled to the top of one of the socks, caught his eye. He stared at it thoughtfully.

'Ah, sure, 'twas maybe worth it all,' he said.

Viciously he ripped off the label, scowling at the shreds of nylon clinging to the metal clip.

'Virtue must not go unrewarded,' he said. 'We'll see that you get a medal for life-saving from some quarter or another.'

At these words, Byrne jumped to his feet. He crossed to where McGill and Clancy were sitting and gazed down at them sternly.

'What are the pair of you planning?' he asked the upturned, astonished faces. 'Fair is fair, you know. Any medals that are going should come my way. Only for I had

37

the presence of mind to throw myself at —' he pointed dramatically, '— Tom here, he would have been swept away. It was my weight kept his feet on the ground.'

Normal Procedure

EITHNE STRONG

'I hate being circumscribed,' Miss Gormley said out loud towards the cage. The balding magpie in it answered in its way. Miss Gormley was wearing green tights and a longish narrow skirt with a slit up the side. She had been wearing the same skirt the previous day when the Dean had brought up the matter of appearance at the staff meeting. It had been one of her more obviously braless days also. They had been becoming more frequent latterly.

Miss Gormley told visitors she did not keep the bird as a pet. She ached for the poor thing, she would say. The cage was the lesser of two evils, the second of course being death.

At the meeting a certain obliquity regarding moral standards had slipped in among the other straight items. The Dean had emphasized that the school, categorically, was not the sort of place where a particular kind of whistle from a boy might go unreprimanded. Castigation of the exciting causes of such a whistle was left almost totally to inference. The Dean had gone on to stress the necessity for the inculcation and preservation of decorum as a counter to unsavoury trends everywhere threatening.

The bird Miss Gormley had found, a maimed fledgling. She had refuged it, tended its hurt, and by the time it was mended it carried the taint of captivity and could not be allowed loose among the predatory hazards of the urban trees. The man who lived with her that month happened to have, among other unlikely oddments, a Victorian parrot-cage. He gave it to her. She also gave him favours, lightly bestowed.

The parrot-cage and Miss Gormley's care combined did not add up to natural processes and the magpie, although cheerful, was undersized and poorly feathered.

Miss Gormley continued talking towards the bird, 'So I'll damn their eyes again.' As she said it she was pulling a tight sweater over her naked top half. 'I'm off,' she said to the man, reading, still bedded on the mattress. She leant across him to snatch an opened fan from its slanted arrangement on the wall. 'I'm taking this for them to draw today,' she said. 'Have something nice — lasagne and chianti, say — ready for me. I'll be starving. Today is my longest day, remember?'

'You'll get fat,' he said. He was a dark heavy man.

'No fear . . . anyway I can afford to. So make it lasagne.'

'What'll you do for all these comforts when I'm gone, next week?'

'By then I'll be due a change. By then it will be time to sample someone else's cuisine.'

She delayed a second by the door looking back at him. He did not appear to give her any of his attention. 'I'm just off,' she repeated, 'but first I'll hang the cage outside — or maybe you might do it for me?'

He said, 'I saw some perfect specimens of her kind dive-bombing the cage yesterday. They hate the ragged creature that she is. For her difference. As far as those free proud ones are concerned she is a deviant. They are entirely true to instinct. Survival demands destruction, obliteration, of a functionless deviance, of a defective member. Or what appears to be such.'

'You may be quite right.' She said it airily. 'In the mean-time the poor thing needs, at least, the air, if that is about all of her natural condition she can have. Hang her out, will you?' She got no further comeback and she said, but quite amiably, 'Oh you . . . I'll put it out myself.' She swung the heavy cage onto a wall hook outside the window. Quickly then she caught up a striped straw bag wherein were some of the things of her trade. On top of them she dropped the fan and hurried out of the room.

But she did not get out of the house immediately. Mrs Baily was in the hall. 'I am actually going, Miss Gormley,' she said. A small travelling-case was at her feet. She went on in little flurries, 'Amazing, isn't it, that I have actually managed it? I have said goodbye to her. I give her the best of my life. What I mean is the best I possibly can. In the ten years of her life I have never taken a day off with peace, as I've often told you.' The young blind girl she was talking about went past Miss Gormley, her elbows angled outwards while with hands sensing the space before her she made her way upstairs. 'And now I'm actually going . . . for over a week.'

Miss Gormley said nothing for a while. She looked up the stairs to where the girl's older brother stood on the landing. As his sister came close to the spot where he was he turned his head away and when her searching hand came near him he moved back to the wall. Miss Gormley said then, 'I should have thought time off was essential. Surely there are places to take care of her while you get away?'

'There are — is — there's the Institute. But I always have these worries, these anxieties about her. I know, I know . . . you'll call me what everyone else does . . .' Mrs Baily fluttered an unhappy hand towards the ceiling, '. . . neurotic. All right. But I'm going away now for a week and . . . I have fixed up things. I've said goodbye. Goodbye again Tom!' This to the boy above them. '. . . and the taxi is to be here in a minute — in fact it *is* here.' The slam of a car door was to be heard outside. 'Goodbye again, Tom.' The boy still gave no word but watched her go, his narrow face out of the light. Miss Gormley also called goodbye in her fashion and then rushed along.

The Dean was not a fat man. When he was anywhere juxtaposed with people of either sex whose swelling flesh was conspicuous his celibate features took on an extra reserve. One might infer from his face at those times that such manifestation of the human shape was an offence, even an obscenity. Energy in any burgeoning form appeared to upset him. His function was one of control and under his jurisdiction energy was required to operate within the framework of his prescription. The special leather implement in his righthand pocket gave witness to his dislike of certain schoolboy departures from that framework.

Miss Gormley saluted him, 'Hello Dean.' It sounded brightly but seemed to be a manner of address to which he did not freely respond. He made his brand of harnessed sound at her as she sped on to the staffroom. There the break

41

was in usual swing. At one end the men talked football and hangovers. At the other, the women were entangled in the matter of black tights.

One teacher was saying flatly, 'I hate them. School stockings finished me with the black.'

'You went to a convent school?' Miss Gormley asked; her air amid them could be said to carry the protection of insouciance.

'Didn't we all?' the first teacher said.

'I love the black ones,' Miss Gormley said, untroubled. She had often been heard referring to the 'experimental' school where she herself had been. 'Especially the see-through sort. They look super with red.'

'Yes, the red-light area.' The teacher pressed close her calves in their safe beige.

'It's a pity the religious life has imbued black with such schizoid connotations.' As Miss Gormley said it she plonked down her bag of Italian dyed straw, and took out the fan which she flicked open, her bright green leg flashing a step or two.

'My God, but you're the giddy girl this day with your St Patrick's Day green.'

'I love colours on the leg. Experimenting,' Miss Gormley insisted.

'And you have the leg for all that too,' one of the men called, distracted from his football.

The class-bell rang and soon the staffroom was empty but for two of the women whose exchanges continued into their free period.

'Our friend Miss Gormley upsets the Dean.'

'She may have another think coming.'

'Of course one allows that art teachers tend to be that bit different but . . .'

'Indeed. You can say that again. I have had the pupils bringing up some of her ideas — in my opinion to nobody's advantage. In fact a number of those in her class were definitely disturbed trying to figure out what she meant by saying the devil is a projection of private and aggregate fantasy.'

'What business has she bringing that sort of rubbish into

42

the art class? I'm certainly glad none of my children have her for anything. Supposing, just by some freak, supposing she got civics to teach, or religion . . . God! Doesn't bear thinking.'

'There is, too, the problem that she lives so close. All the pupils live around. There is nothing to stop any of them knowing . . . She could have the decency to keep herself private.'

'But it's clear she doesn't give a damn what anyone thinks. Actually she even makes a point of . . . well, you could say, . . . brazenness.'

'You have seen the set-up she lives in?'

'Mmm. Who hasn't. She invites the world. No reserve. What most struck me was her way of having everything different from the way any normal person would want it — old water-pipes deliberately laid bare — that sort of thing. She says she likes their *configuration*. And she doesn't go for TV, and she has never understood the need for a fridge in this climate and she has taken down the partition so that the bathroom is actually part of the main room.'

'That's because, as she puts it, she likes to *observe*, have everything open to her, while she relaxes in her bath.'

'She roared laughing the other day when I was telling about our getting the new teak front door. She sets great value on all that old moth-eaten stuff that looks as if it was hauled from God knows where. And then the mattress actually down on the floor. The size of it too! The day I was there she had three boy friends in tow.'

'You know I can't but feel more and more that things should be put to the Dean. Plainly, I mean. We have the right of objection to staff conduct. A standard is required. That sort of irregularity, looseness, is a matter of . . . of . . .'

'Of scandal?'

'Exactly. Not to be countenanced. To be rooted out.'

Miss Gormley walked down the school drive. At the bend of the hill the gate stood open. A tree beside it was splendid, alone and strongly spread. Against the sky its stripped branches, patterning a light stone colour in the March sun, could call to mind a cathedral, not any of the gloom but the aspiration, the triumph of delicately achieved masonry. At the high point of the arched tracery two magpies sat making every few seconds their kind of rattle, a repeating short harshness proclaiming a winter vigorously won and a fresh urgency. The birds gleamed clear health, white and black. From a little way over the roofs, from the unseen hanging cage, an impoverished eager magpie sound came to meet their regenerative insistence. The two handsome creatures rose and flew in sharp spurts to a point above the house where Miss Gormley and Mrs Baily lived and then they both swooped decisively. Miss Gormley suddenly began running down the hill.

When she reached the door she several times missed the keyhole. As she was at last managing to twist the key a large object from somewhere up the wall of the house fell past her. It made a wild terrible cry which made Miss Gormley turn from the door and look downwards. Below her on the basement strip of concrete Mrs Baily's blind daughter lay twisted peculiarly. A whiff of cooking garlic came on the air.

While the ambulance was on its way the child croaked once from under Miss Gormley's shawl, 'Tom . . . did it . . . Tom . . . pushed me out the window.' A good deal later when the girl's broken legs could be left to nurses, Miss Gormley took up her first hurry to the cage. She found the rickety bars strained away at one side. The pecked bloody bundle inside was not yet altogether cold.

The man said, his hands trying to make a beginning and end, '. . . I had gone to get the wine . . .'

Tell Me Once Again
You Love Me

VINCENT LAWRENCE

On that particular evening Hennessy dwelt upon a promontory, far out along a self-inflicted spit of lonely soil, with his trousers' legs tucked into his socks and his mental processes all involuted and turned backwards, towards the past. Or the present. Or the future. For to Hennessy they were all the same, as he never could distinguish between time and tide, or tide and time, or time, tide and the seasons, or when to sow and when to reap, or when to end a daisy-chain, or when to lie back laughing upon the newmown grass. Sometimes he looked inside himself, and was sucked downwards and waylaid by the smugness of his ways, the little comforts, starts and hesitations, the smiles, the easy tears, and the superficial bland acceptance of the fences in his mind.

At other times, and they were numerous too, he reached outwards, towards a tiny speck of light, a roguish pin-prick, behind which lurked, but only possibly, a concatenation of viable responses which might impart assurance to the living of his days. Everything bothered him, and he groaned more often than he cried.

Watch him now as, standing at the window of the classroom, he gazes at great scudding banks of cloud as they chase one another across a late September sky, while outside the people in the street, distraught and windblown, with cold, withdrawn faces, flapping coats and watery eyes, hurry past each other and never even stop to say hello. And Hennessy, for it was his wont to dramatize, imagines on his forehead, like a neon sign, in letters bright and tall, the word Sinner flashing on and off, to catch the interest of the passersby and amaze their stolid evening lives. As if God would bother.

And turning now to see once more those rows and rows of restive little boys, with Jimmy Addams sleeping yet again, sitting only slightly sideways, chin on chest and pencil still in hand, and his quiet smile betokening dreams of smallboy wonder and surprise, far away from schools and dusty learning, with no one there to murmur stop, or here, come back and tie your laces and button up your coat. And you leave him to his slumber, for the clock above the door says five to four, while the room is full of fading daylight, and the wind still blows and nudges at the windows, rustling out a warning to you, of how it will surprise you when you step outside, to come whistling up your underwear and down about your ears, and make you pine for the warmth of the overcoat, which you hocked to M.J. Speed, to enable you to take Miss Molly Church to see O'Toole from Connemara wait around for Godot, who never ever came. Look at all those little boys, how they shift and rustle, tiny creaks and whisperings, in anticipation of release, from a captivity of fulminations, threats of dire retribution, and dull, sad slabs of learning, offered soberly and joylessly, to be gobbled up and stored inside the brain-box, like dead bodies in a morgue. And to what purpose? Why, to enable them to emulate their teachers, and their parents, and their brothers and their sisters, to join the company of faceless people, with slack imaginations and no great need to wonder, if roses and their like do indeed bloom in the dark. So sad.

So Hennessy loping round the room, he too awaiting his release, for he's a prisoner of the system also, which says that there shall be no end, and no beginning either, there shall only be continuance, each face and each awakening heart a link in the fragile chain, which binds a structure based on order and decorum, and a damping down of instinct, thought, and feeling; a structure which forms lovely little men and women, who welcome in the old traditions, and are borne back ceaselessly, on the silent flowing river of mediocrity and sameness, in Ireland now. For you know you're right, and everybody else is wrong, but it is lonely sitting gazing at a wall, and seeing it, when you could much more easily give up, give in, nod and smile, clasp a hand and hold it, and say, Tell me once again you love me, just once more.

But surely time has no dominion then or now, as Jimmy Addams may awake, and as if he'd caused it, the bell begins to ring. The usual gabbled prayer, the boys file out like notes of music down a page, and Hennessy wanders down the corridor, to the staffroom and the company of Martin Savage, a small man, with a small man's eager energy, where he sits whistling on the corner of a table, surrounded by a cornucopia of aging textbooks, uncorrected exercises, coloured brochures, mildewed notices of half-forgotten rules, and the remains of his lunch.

'Let there be no surrender, only the strong shall inherit the earth.'

'When I'm taken, I want it to be in a flaming chariot, with two comely angels to hold me down, and a third to whisper in my ear, to tell me that I'd only got what I deserved.'

'There'll be no remorse. Nothing has any meaning, and no one will be saved. We won't even go together, we'll go singly, or in pairs of strangers, and woe betide those who come from north of the Liffey.'

'Shall we dance?'

And out they go, in stiff-backed, close formation, down the corridor, past the muddy footballers tiptoeing in like late arriving husbands, then with averted faces close beside the office of the Principal, that well-meaning man, and the glass doors of the main entrance softly puff behind them like the echo of a sigh. Goodbye.

To survey the weathered face of the heavens, and a flight of swallows darting swiftly, fading over rooftops clear against the darkening sky, and hurrying now along the seafront, in the company of this little man from Galway, Hennessy imagines a half-remembered throbbing in his head, a sense of something barely like elation, as if all the juices of his body, and his mind, were coalescing. For tonight, like every night, Miss Molly Church awaits you, in the light and warmth and brightness, of Harry Fenton's snug in Grafton Street, that lively, pulsing girl with autumn hair, whose face and outward aspect sing a song within the hearts of all who know her, for she is in truth a gorgeous creature, and you love her now and then. Passing in the large green bus the spray-whipped length of the Bull Wall, you dream about the long hot summer days, and the little town of Wexford where you met her, the narrow streets through which she moved before you knew her, how you envied them their knowledge of her form and grace, and her silver surge of laughter, like sparkling wine stirred up within a crystal glass. Now by Fairview, and its silent cold deserted park, and the smell of the river, hanging like a fetid curtain between the gusts of wind; and you remember silver beech, and flickering aspen leaves, which shake because Christ said they should, and sunbursts of flowers in meadows of long grass, where you lay, and let the long day roll towards evening, and the slow measured tone of bells, their timbre quivering through the balmy air, gave rhythm to your hands, as they brushed against her face, but she would not let you kiss her, and she cried because you did not persevere. As the bus rolls towards the Five Lamps, and speeds along the North Strand, how you feel the slow rise of longing beat within your heart, and yet when you descend at Dawson Street you drag your feet and follow Savage when he beckons to you, and you both fade furtively into the cool cavernous depths of Swanson's public bar and grill. Thirstily.

And behold, here's H.B. Toft, the Dublin poet, long and thin, with hair like thistledown, and a long stream of heavy sounding clichés falling effortlessly from his wet mouth. In the quiet sheen of light, how the glasses and the bottles glimmer, and the old, well-polished chairs and tables lend their burnished brown benignity, as a gracious gift, to the restfulness and comfort of the place. So Hennessy smiles, and ducks his head, and commands the aged barman to produce some foaming tankards of the native dark brown ale, while the noble, drunken poet weaves an aureole of wordplay, as he talks of brown knees dusted with a coating of Jurassic sand, and how once upon a time, some towers bloomed, and died, in Samarkand. And now that lovely girl beside you inclines her glossy head, and raises high her cool white hand, with fingers long and slender, to sip her portion of Drambuie, oh so gracefully, with a minimum of effort and no small amount of skill.

'I beg your pardon, could you just? . . .'
'Could I just what?'
'Could you just remain like that a moment longer?'
'If it's absolutely necessary.'
'I assure you, yes, it is.'

'Are you an artist?'

'No, my name is Hennessy, I pretend to be a man of leisure.'

'Really?'

'Really.'

'What are you really?'

'I'm afraid.'

'Afraid? Afraid of what?'

'Of you. Of me. Of everything. Don't you know me?'

'No, I don't. Who are you?'

'I'm the voice that might speak to you of deliverance, that might tell you of free space and of floating visibly or invisibly, as you like, towards a continuum of silence felt but not heard, perhaps along the heartstrings, or in the quivering of your very being. Yesterday, or was it today? I dined with Mary Tubman . . .'

'Mary Tubman?'

'A fine upstanding woman from the bottom of our street.'

'I can't say that I've heard of her.'

'Nor she of you?'

'Possibly.'

'Or probably.'

And Hennessy turns to smile about him, at the glaze of tosspot faces, while the sturdy length of poet rolls his coloured balloons of rhythms round the walls, bouncing them as amber emanations against the variegated glinting of the bottles and the glasses near and far. Oh Hennessy, how you love these people, these surroundings; how you glory so vicariously in the reflected light of learning, to be like them, to be so godlike and so cultured, to have nothing of the mundane world to ever, ever touch you, and to have someone there beside you, to be the mirrored doppelganger of your fondest felt imaginings of yourself. Fool! For when Hennessy grips the slim, white hand, which has been feeling up his vitals, he discovers, to his shame and his chagrin, that he's been playing tip and tickle with the poet's latest boy-friend, a sixteen-year-old wilted lettuce, who sports hair the hue of custard, and has a smile like the ladder in a stocking, all down the length of his sad face.

So with a sigh you rise, amid a sea of shushings, to disturb the status quo, and tell Toft that he's a fraud, and that he's talking syncopated rubbish, and you abuse them all, those milk and cream Olympians, with the ignorance of your ways. Thou turd.

But you shall suffer for your temerity, for see the shaggy-headed poet, as he rolls his eyeballs and his sleeves, how with one breathless surge of motion, he bounces Hennessy, instead of rhythms, down the stairs, and out, onto bum-freezing concrete, and Dawson Street, and night. Sic gloria transit this thing.

Shall you shed a tear as you recline, with no pillow for your head, and no hint of sky above you, but a starry sign which enjoins you to Beware the Wrath of God? Assuredly not. This is not the time for weeping, not the time for sad or black despairs, for the night is fraught with possibilities, intimations of the shades of other dreamers, fools and vagabonds, who traipsed and scuttled in the wake of silver shining wonders embedded rakishly in the wasteland of their souls. For you know one thing, and you hold it to be true, that if tradition trails a structure of conformity, then what matters is coherence as a fabric whole and clear; but you know one other thing, and you also hold it to be true, that the stars that shine in Miss Molly Church's eyes are farther from you than the nearest one, of those that wink now in the firmament above you. And you remember once again the sinecure of her body, all aplay with light and shade, how it teases with its symmetry, how it blesses all and every gaze, but how it also shies away from all palpation, and dimples into merriment, and thus preserves the wonder of its secret places, from the aching vulnerability of your own rude hands. Which only seek to tell her how you love her, both her body and her mind, but especially her body, for her mind hides no complexities, as it merely dwells in sunlight, and in happiness and laughter, and banishes all else. For ever?

So see Hennessy as he collects the pieces of his shattered wits, and leans them bit by bit against the wall of Saltby's cake and coffee shop, how he yearns for invisibility, to range the width of the wide and waking world, as a free spirit; to peer with no little interest into deep, dark wells of sentience, which by extension might admit a magnanimity of

consciousness, which is severely to be wished. In the darkness
of the night, with people passing by who know nothing of
the yearning in your heart. Nor wish to. How to reach them?
How to delve beneath the outward, placid surface, and let
them really see you care. But do you care? Ah, Hennessy, do
you really care? And you remember how once you had
a vision, how it came upon you suddenly as an act of
revelation, peopling your universe with phantoms, and the
deep, dark silent laughter of the shades of what had gone,
and what would surely come, if, hearing people tap upon
your skull, you allowed them in, to reside with you, in an
helminthiasis which would be beyond recall. For you beheld,
beneath a bloodred setting sun, a glaring cliff face crumbling
into soft and sodden clay, and the hard and noble lines of the
buildings of a city melting and becoming merely dust, while
over all a child held out its chubby fist, demanding with its
crying voice that it should be protected and held fast, in the
midst of a faint dissolving universe, and like a fool, you
alone reached out your hand, presumptuously. For you
know there is no basis for communication, no easy spring-
board towards the understanding of your fellow man, and
was it not the Greeks who gave to will the confining bonds of
reason, and so laid down a groundwork of convention and
tradition, with the proper words and gestures all defined, and
afterwards refined and polished into a comforting familiarity,
by succeeding generations, so that something that might once
have possibly been simple, has become absurd. And yet love
is still such a little word.

And Hennessy shakes his head, as he stands trapped within
the cavern of the streets of Dublin, while overhead the sky
shows fitfully that the night is still not far advanced, perhaps
it's only still about the stroke of midnight, and then indeed
the bells of Christchurch, and St Patrick's too, take up the
clarion call and proclaim, as their chimes roll joyously across
the ancient city, that time has once more broken through.
Now the pubs disgorge their hosts of young and old imbibers,
who gather into animated groups, as if reluctant to lose
contact with the loud and false companionship, and the
alcoholic daze induced by Cork gin and Paddy whiskey,
washed down by foaming pints of Guinness stout, to the

manner born. While from the darkness of his doorway Hennessy sticks out a furtive head, and his anxious eyes slide quickly past innumerable brown paper parcels, held firm beneath the oxters, as he scans the faces of the revellers, for a sign of Martin Savage, or a glimpse of any other physiognomy, which might show a speck of friendliness, and so relieve the burden of his guilt-infested haze.

'Good evening, brother.'

'Jesus Christ!'

'Not he, brother. But I carry his message.'

'No fooling?'

'Beware the wrath of God.'

'I've had word already.'

'It bears repeating, brother. The ungodly must be punished.'

'Tell me more.'

'Give ear, O heavens, and I will speak; and let the earth hear the words of my mouth.'

'I'm all agog.'

'May my teaching drop as the rain, my speech distil as the dew, as the gentle rain upon the tender grass, and as the showers upon the herb.'

'Hallelujah.'

'For I will proclaim the name of the Lord. Ascribe greatness to our God!'

'You've never lost it.'

'I will make my arrows drunk with blood, and my sword shall devour flesh — with the blood of the slain and the captives, from the long-haired heads of the enemy.'

'Could you keep it down just a little? You see . . .'

'Let it ring out, brother. The enemy is all about. He is the tall, dark man who lurks in byways; he is as insidious as the stain upon the bedsheet, as the hand that writes in lavatories; and he descends upon his prey as coldly and as silently as the fog upon the mountain top. He tantalizes with his honeyed words, with the lubricity of his ways; causing young maidens to feel the dew between their soft, pneumatic thighs . . .'

'Stop it Henry. You're making me randy.'

'Let it all hang out, brother. Cleanse yourself this night by indulgence in debauchery, and so awake tomorrow a holier

52

and a wiser man.'

'Lead on, lead on . . .'

And he takes off: Henry Farmer, gaunt and long in sack-cloth britches, a professional, impressionistic tramp, who stands outside the Shelbourne Hotel like an avenging angel, and frightens timid people into giving him handouts, not to mention the odd piece of discarded raiment, on nights when jollity descends into out and out conviviality of the worst sort. So they both breast the night-time, chilly winds of Baggot Street, Farmer and Hennessy, Hennessy and Farmer, the procurer and procured, while the city sings to them a song of wickedness, of lewdness and laughter, and the joyous wild abandonment of values only skin-deep held, by a catholicity of Catholics, by staunch and upright Irishmen, and by hordes of maternal would-be mothers whose maiden-heads must not be broken, only bent.

And Hennessy begins to feel once more, along his nerve ends and in the shadowiest hollows of his heart, the stirrings of a little something, not hope, but rather . . . expectation: a rebuttal, a denial of what has gone before, not of life, or the living of it, but a negation of the trappings and the artifice, of the scheming and the scrambling, and the awful empty words and gestures which masquerade as empathy, and in fact sow seeds of further discontents. Deep within him now he imagines that he can discern a nugget, a golden vein of spontaneity, which will rise and greet, like the dawning of a summer morning, the simplicity that surely must exist beneath the layers of methodology, and so enable him to see Miss Molly Church for what she is, and not for what he imagines that she should be. What a shit the man is!

Now by gleaming canal water they make their way, while the wind riddles patterns of dead leaves about their feet, and the clouds play hop-scotch with the moon, dissolving surfaces into kaleidoscopes of swirling images, into wavering outlines of insubstantial greys and blacks, so that movement crawls and billows everywhere, and lends a glaucomatous unreality to all the place about. Across the bridge and past the massive locks, where in summer sun the children often sport and sometimes drown, and where the spirit of the tired old poet, perhaps, is still inclined to wander, enclosed forever in the warmth and beauty of his verse. Then Leeson Street unfolds its length before them, a trackless waste of dilapidated Georgian mansions, with tiny windows high above them winking light, from little rooms, where eighteen-year-old typists, secretaries and students, civil servants and fledgling school teachers, people from the country and people from the towns, from Cork and Galway, Clare and Donegal, dwell alone in a pale solitude, listening to hear each other breathe.

Is it really so, you wonder, as you scurry through the night, can hope forever be eluded, can the mirror image be avoided, can the whispering voice be stilled; and the self-hugging vulnerability and opaqueness of your vision makes you almost wish to scream. While you follow Henry Farmer, through the tortured autumn darkness, round a corner, down a ringing set of metal stairs, until the knock upon the door admits you both to a long hallway, and the pyrexia and claustrophobic atmosphere of the subterranean apartment, which Madame Mary Tubman calls her home.

Ah, the wonder of it all, as light distilled through water converges and withdraws, in trochilic combinations of jungle green, Lincoln green, sea green, bottle green, pea; an aquamarine world, through which swim both the people and the fish, with pulsing gills and bulging eyeballs, whether in the tanks or out, and Mary Tubman waving welcome, in a graceful sign language of slow motion, like a lardy sea-queen of the depths. For they are all present, all the gaudy, raddled girls, and Billy Cream, the juggler, Marcie Whitman and her pearls, Martin Savage, Janice Waterman, O'Rooney and his dog, Miss Molly Church, Professor Rafferty, McOyster and McJones, and poor old lonely Gunnerswasp, attired in his dunce's hat, and standing in the corner, far away from this or any other world.

What a noble sight, thinks Hennessy, as having undergone a sea-change, he meets up with Father Tim, the silent priest, who conveys his thoughts by means of little notes, scribbled on the official pad provided, and passed coyly to the recipient, accompanied by a simpering wish to please. And as you take the sweaty notepaper, and avert your head to hide your anguished smile, suddenly you think of all the lonely places, all the nooks and crannies of the mind, where men, and women too, retreat in search of refuge, and a little peace, far away from past observances, and unsought responsibilities, solid dreams and hard-edged, brittle tears, places which do not in fact exist, not now, or ever. For it seems that they, unlike you, still have not seen, or understood, that the course is forward: there is no going back. Tell them, Hennessy, how it is, and how it will ever be, when there will be no more brakeshoes on their minds, and how they can rise to the same level of performance as Father Tim, who can do it in a hammock, as his note proclaims. What a man!

And Hennessy permits himself to move a little to the left of centre, or is it to the right, to where Miss Molly Church must always seem to be, that soft and gentle girl, in her long, dewy sheen of innocence, but muted, never shattering the stillness of her inviolability, and where at times she might appear, to other, less adoring eyes, to fade into the background, and become part, not alone of the scenery, but even of the very furnishings of her surroundings, like an exquisite frieze or pattern caught and held in amber. What a pity it would be to have her speak, so instead you strike a note, a pinging echo from your glass, which causes all activity within that swirling room to cease, even to the fish within their tanks. Did you really mean to let it happen, must you rob your mind so quickly of its wandering, are you now in fact bereft of . . . what?

While Jimmy Addams swims back into your vision, still fast asleep and happy, and why should he not be, for the clock still stands at five to four, and the early autumn darkness has made no further inroads, and the world still hums and whistles on its ordinary course. And you wonder at your temerity, how your mind presumed to linger, all down the space of one long moment, forsaking those calm and silent shores, where sanity prevails, and greyness is the colour, and time the metronome.

So Hennessy retreats once more, out onto the very tip of that same promontory, which lurks within the secret places, the windy, desolate barrenness of his heart's core, there to stagnate, while his other self, his outward bold exterior, will doff his hat, raise his hand, wave and proceed jauntily towards a future of Miss Molly Church, and children, and money in the bank, and a merging of minds which will lend security to all his length of days.

In a pig's arse, Hennessy, in a pig's arse.

Skin

NEIL JORDAN

The odd fantasies we people our day with. She had just pierced her fingers with the knife and from between the petals of split skin, blood was oozing. It was coming in one large drop, growing as it came. Till her detached face was reflected in the crimson.

But in fact the knife had missed her forefinger. It had cut round the gritty root of the lopped-off stem and was now splicing the orb into tiny segments. Her eyes were running. Cracked pieces of onion spitting moisture at her, bringing tears, misting her view of the enamel sink. And the sink was, despite the distortion of tears, as stolidly present as it had been yesterday.

She was absorbed in the onion's double-take; its deceit. She had peeled layer upon layer from it and was anticipating a centre. Something like a fulcrum, of which she could say: here the skin ends; here the onion begins. And instead there was this endless succession of them, each like a smaller clenched fist, fading eventually into insignificance; embryonic, cell-like tissue which gave the appearance of a core. But in fact it was the same layers, in miniature. Ah, she sighed, almost disappointed, looking at the handful of diced onion on the draining-board. She gathered the pieces in her hands and shook them into the bowl. Then she washed her hands to dispel the damp, oily feeling, the acid smell. And she turned her back on the sink, then gazed absently on the kitchen table.

She had an apron on her, something like a smock. Flowers bloomed on it, toy elephants cavorted on their hind legs. There was a bow-tied string at the back and a slit-pocket across the front in which she could place her hands or dry her fingers. Above it her face, which was uneventfully trim, and just a little plain. She was wearing high-heeled house slippers and an over-tight bra. Her shoulder was shifting uncomfortably because of it. When one rests one notices such things. She was resting. From the diced onions, carrots, chunks of meat, whole potatoes on the draining-board. From the black and white pepper tins on the shelf above it.

There were two large windows on the sink side of the room. On the wall opposite was a row of small single-pane windows, high up, near the roof. The midday sun came streaming in the large window from behind her. She saw it as a confluence of rays emanating from her. When she shifted, even her shoulder, there would be a rapid rippling of light and shadow on the tablecloth. Blue light it was, reflecting the blueness of the kitchen decor. For everything was blue here, the pantry door, the dresser, the walls were painted in rich emulsion, varying from duck egg to cobalt. And the day was a mild early September with a sky that retained some of August's scorched vermilion. The image of the Virgin's blue mantle crossed her silent, vacant eyes. She had raised her hand to her hair and saw the light break through the fingers. She thought of the statue in the hall; plastic hands with five plastic sun rays affixed to each; streaming towards the feet, the snake, the water-bowl. Mother of Christ.

She had been humming the first phrases of a tune. She stopped it when she returned abruptly to the sink, to the window, to the strip of lard — sparrow meat — hanging outside. She chopped the meat into neat quarters and dumped them, with the meat and vegetables, into a saucepan. She placed the saucepan on a slowburning ring. Then she began washing her hands again. The scent of onion still clung to them. Pale hands, made plump by activity, swelling a little round the wrist and round the spot where the tarnished engagement ring pulled the flesh ·inwards. She massaged separately the fingers of each hand, rapidly and a little too harshly, as if she were vexed with them, trying to coax something from them. Their lost freshness.

Several inches of water in the sink; a reflection there — two hands caressing, a peering face swimming in the mud-coloured liquid, strewn over with peel. She grabbed hold of the knife and plunged it, wiping it clean with her bare thumb and forefinger. And again came the image — blood oozing, in large crimson drops. But her finger didn't gape. The knife

58

emerged clean.

She pulled the sink plug then, hearing the suck, scouring the residue of grit and onion-skin with her fingers. She dried her hands, walking with the towel into the living room.

There, there was a low-backed modern sofa, two older tattered armchairs and a radiogram piled with magazines. She sat in the sofa, easing herself into its cushioned supports. She fiddled with the radio dial, turned it on, heard one blare of sound and switched it off again. The silence struck her; the chirp of a sparrow outside, clinging to the strip of lard. In another minute she was restless again, leafing through the magazines, flicking impatiently over their pages.

A housewife approaching middle-age. The expected listlessness about the features. The vacuity that suburban dwelling imposes, the same vacuity that most likely inhabited the house next door. But she was an Irish housewife, and as with the whole of Irish suburbia, she held the recollection of a half-peasant memory fresh and intact. Noticeable in her dealings with the local butcher. She would bargain, oblivious of the demands of propriety. She would talk about childhood with an almost religious awe, remembering the impassioned innocence of her own. And, although house-proud, rigorous tidiness made her impatient; she had a weakness for loose ends.

And in her the need for the inner, secret life still bloomed. It would come to the fore in odd moments. A fragment of a song, hummed for a bar or two, then broken off. A daydream. She would slip into it like a suicide easing himself into an unruffled canal. She would be borne off, swaying, for a few timeless moments. She would hardly notice the return. And, during occasional stark flashes she would be seized by a frightening admixture of religious passion and guilt, bordering on a kind of painful ecstasy; the need, the capacity for a religiously intense experience of living; and in consequence of the lack of this, a deep residue of guilt. At times like this she would become conscious of anything red and bloodlike, and anything blue or bright, any play of light upon shade.

But if she were asked how she lived she would have replied: happily. And if she were asked what happiness meant she wouldn't even have attempted an answer.

She found herself rummaging among the magazines, searching out one she had been reading yesterday. She recalled a story in it about the habits of Swedish housewives. Certain of them who would drive from their homes between the idle hours of two and four in the afternoon, out to the country, and there offer themselves to men. The event would take place in a field, under a tree, in a car. And afterwards, they would straighten their clothes, return home to find the timing-clock on the oven at nought, the evening meal prepared. It had disgusted her thoroughly at first glance. But something in it had made her read to the finish. The image, perhaps, of a hidden garden, sculpted secretly out of the afternoon hours, where flowers grew with unimaginable freedom.

Now she was feeling the same compulsion. *Circles* was the name, she remembered, selecting one from the pile. She opened it at the centre page. A glaring headline there, in vulgar black print:

'Swedish Housewives' Afternoon Of Sin'

And a picture: a woman standing by a clump of trees, in a shaded country lane. A man in the distance watching her. A parked car.

She closed it instantly. It had disgusted her again. But as she sat there, the sound of distant cars coming to her from the road, her fingers began drumming impatiently on the wooden top of the radio. Something about it drew her. The sun, the glossy green of the foliage. The man's dark, predatory back. Not the cheapness, the titillating obscenity. Not that.

Then she was moving towards the front door. Her tweed walking coat was hanging in the alcove. Outside, rows of starlings laced the telegraph-wires. Motionless black spearheads, occasionally breaking into restless, wheeling flights, to return again to their rigid formations. Expectant beakheads against a waning skyline. The same expectant stasis in her, her drumming fingers like their fluttering wings. She was a starling. The sudden, unconscious burst of disquiet. The animal remembrances of a home more vibrant, more total than this one. The origin-trek; the ache for aliveness.

All the way through the hall, out the front door, her fingers drummed. As she turned the ignition-key in the dashboard, the engine's purr seemed to echo this drumming.

Howth was facing her as she drove, bringing to her a desperate need for open spaces. Slim, spearlike poplars passed on her left. Oak, gnarled and knotted to bursting point. Ash and elder, their autumn leaves discoloured by traffic dust. She drove mechanically. She hardly noticed the line of cars coming towards her. Only the earth, to her left, sodden under the weight of fallen leaf. The sea to her right, a dull metal plate today. Beyond it, as if thrusting at its horizon with a giant closed hand, the Hill of Howth.

Her forefinger still tapping on the steering wheel. Scrubbing vegetables had banished most of the varnish from the nail. Today she didn't see it. A car swerved into her lane and away. She had a moment's vision of herself as a bloodied doll, hanging through a sharded windscreen. She drew a full breath and held it, her lungs like a balloon, pressing at her breasts.

She pulled in at a causeway that led across marshlands to the open sea. She quenched the engine and gave herself time to absorb the shock of silence. Then she opened the door, got out, her fingers drumming on the metal roof.

Sounds that could have been grass unbending or scurrying insects came to her. The lapping hiss of tide from the marshlands; its necklace of canals. But now she was here, she wasn't sure why she had come. What to do with 'this' — as if the scene before her was a kind of commodity. The sheer expansiveness of silence.

She ran from the car door to the edge of the causeway in an attempt at the abandonment she imagined one should feel. There was a drop there, then mud-flats awaiting tide. Nothing came of it. Only the sense of her being a standing, awkward thing among grasses that crept, tides that flowed. The alternative — to lie, to open her ears reclining, to roughen her cheeks with ragwort and sea-grass didn't occur to her. She began to walk.

There were ships, tankers most likely, on the rim of the sea. As she walked through the burrows she saw hares bound-

61

ing. She noticed the sun, weak but still potent. She saw a single lark spiralling towards it. She saw, when she reached it, a restful strand dissolve on either side into the autumn haze. It was empty of people.

The sand rose in flurries with her steps. She had worn the wrong shoes: those high-heeled slippers. Useless, she thought, slipping them off to carry them.

The sea amazed her when she reached it. Surging, like boiling green marble. Very high too, from yesterday's spring tide. There was a swell, beginning several yards out, that reached her in ripples. Each wave seemed to rise like a solid thing, laced with white foam, subsiding just when she felt it would engulf her. Swelling, swelling, then retreating. The sun glistening coldly off it. She felt wet spray on her cheek; ice cold, like the feel of the green-and-white altar-rail at church.

She decided to risk a paddle. She glanced round her and saw nothing but a black dot, like a rummaging dog, in the distance. So she opened her coat, hitched up her skirt and unpeeled her stockings. She didn't want them wet. She threw them, with her slippers, to a spot she judged safe from the incoming tide. She walked in, delighted with the tiny surging ripples round her ankles. Her feet were soon blue with the cold. She remembered her bad circulation, and vowed not to stay long. But the freshness of it! The clean, salt wetness, up around her calves now! It deserved more than just an ankle-paddle. And soon she was in it up to her knees, with the rim of her skirt all sodden. The green living currents were running about her legs, the rivers of white, puffy foam surrounding her like a bridal wreath. She hitched up her dress then, the way young girls do, tucking it under their drawers to look like renaissance princes, and felt the cold mad abandon of wind and spray on her legs. A wave bigger than the others surged up, wetting her belly and thighs, taking her breath away. The feel of it, fresh and painful, icy and burning! But it was too much, she decided. At her age, skirt tucked up in an empty sea.

She turned to the strand and saw a man there, a wet-tailed cocker-spaniel at his heels, bounding in a flurry of drops. She froze. He had seen her, she was sure, though his eyes were now on the dog beside him. The sight of his tan

62

overcoat and his black oiled hair brought a desolate panic to her. The shame, she thought, glancing wildly around her for stockings and shoes.

But the sea must have touched her core with its irrational, ceaseless surging. For what she then did was to turn again, back to the sea, picking high, delicate steps through its depths, thinking: he sees me. He sees my legs, my tucked-up skirt, the outline of my waist clearly through the salt-wet fabric. He is more excited than I am, being a man. And there was pounding, pounding through her body saying: This is it. This is what the sea means, what it all must mean. And she stood still, the sea tickling her groin, her eyes fixed on the distant tanker, so far off that its smokestack seemed a brush-stroke on the sky, its angular shape that of a flat, painted object; around it the million dulled glimmering mirrors.

But she was wrong. And when she eventually turned she could see the man only as an outline, like the boat, the cocker-spaniel beside him a flurrying black ball. Ah, she thought, I was wrong about that too. And she walked towards the shore, heavy with the knowledge of days unpeeling in layers, her skirt and pants sagging with their burden of water.

A Cow in the House

BENEDICT KIELY

There was something different and a little disconcerting about Harry the Barber, possibly because he drank and had a red face and his hand shook and he kept a cow in the house. The only other man I had ever heard of who kept animals in his dwelling place was a one-eyed, story-book giant who lived in a cave and came to a bad end. So I went cold all over the Friday morning my mother told me to trot down the town to Harry's and take fourpence with me and ask him to trim my hair. Up to that fatal moment, when manhood opened before me like an abyss, my mother herself had done what barbering I needed: combing, snipping and trimming while I, my eyes tightly closed against detached, descending hairs, and robed, like a pantomine Bedouin, in a bath towel, stood on a kitchen chair.

I pleaded, 'Couldn't you trim my hair yourself? You did it last Saturday.'

'You're big enough now to need a real barber. You're like a rabbit hiding under a bush.'

The giant had roared loudly enough to shatter the roof when the burning stake plunged into his only eye.

I said, 'Harry the Barber keeps a cow in the house.'

'Isn't he the lucky man to have a cow?'

'Wouldn't you like to go with your father,' she said, 'and see the capital city and visit Sister Barbara in the Nazareth Home?'

My mother was all flour. That's how I knew so well it was Friday morning for Friday morning was three things: our big weekly baking, particularly of treacle scones which my father loved; the busiest milk delivery day at the co-operative creamery up the road past our house; the day they shod cartwheels across the road and below our terrace on the space of waste ground before Hamilton's smithy. My mother, white as a snowman, stood baking at a table where she could look out of a kitchen window and see the farmers' carts, laden with jingling silvery cans, passing up and down the road; and see the smoke and steam rising as the red-hot metal hoops were fitted onto the wooden wheels and then cooled and contracted with cold water.

The three Hamiltons were giants of men: the white-headed father, the tall dark-visaged sons with deep creases in their faces to catch and hold the smoke and soot of the forge. They swung and stooped over the ancient process, setting alight the circle of peat around the iron hoop, blowing the flames with hand-bellows, dragging out with a huge tongs the sparkling crimson circle, fitting it to the wood and skilfully applying the rhythmical hammers. But they had six kind eyes between them and they didn't keep cows in the smithy. They had a horse but they kept him decently, housed, bedded and cleaned out, in a stable in Tansey the carter's yard at the end of the town.

My mother laid the foundations for yet another scone. The carts shone and jingled up and down the road. Smoke of singed wood, and steam from the cooled iron arose like a mushroom.

So, for all those reasons, it was Friday morning, but for me the light had gone out of the sunshine. Inching towards the door I said, 'I'll go look at the Hamiltons.'

'You'll go off to Harry the Barber's for a new hairstyle. Don't you want to see the capital city of Ireland? Your father says it's time you saw a bit of the world.'

'I saw it all in school. It's a shiny round ball. It spins when you touch it.'

'You're too clever for your years.'

But, in spite of the flour, I could see she was proud of my wit; and I was wise enough to know that going to the capital meant a long glorious journey by train and something to boast about for life. No boy in Primer, which was my grade at school, had ever been farther in a train than the mere forty miles to the sea at Bundoran. Between me and the delights of the long journey to Dublin stood the monster I must pass: the shaking red-faced barber and the cow that would startlingly step out of the hall-door. There was nothing for it but to close my eyes and fare forward. By ill luck

I didn't wear my cap.

A cow's floppy cloven hooves were never made for a hard pavement. Slithering clumsily, the brown-and-white creature emerged and crossed the footwalk to the street. The shop door closed behind her and the bell fixed at the top of it jangled. To my alarm she swung her head sideways and looked at me out of enormous eyes. She had a crumpled horn, like the cow that was milked by the maiden all forlorn, and wisps of hay which she was champing at, meditatively, stuck out of the corners of her mouth and wiggled like cats' whiskers. No maiden, forlorn or otherwise, drove the beast from the byre in the barber's backyard to the pasture at the edge of the town. But behind her walked one of the barber's children: a ragged boy with close-cropped head, and trousers that had once belonged to an elder brother and, cut down and all, were still too big for him. The inexpert retailoring made him look as if one of his buttocks was twice the size of the other. He made hup-hup noises. He poked with an ash twig at the animal's flank. He grandly ignored me; and I was too absorbed by the mystery of the cow that used the shop door to think twice about the significance of that little cropped head. Clutching my fourpence and facing up to fate, I pushed open the door. The same bell rang to herald my entrance that had rung to tell of the departure of the cow.

Harry the Barber was saying, 'It's kinda awkward at times. You'd be amazed how some people are affected when she walks in one door and out the other. But the only other exit is to make her swim the river at the bottom of the yard.'

'You've no back entrance,' said one of the two customers. He had two gold teeth and talked through his nose.

'Nor exit,' said Harry.

'The town,' said the second customer, 'isn't much of a place for a cow or a collie dog.' He was a mountainy farmer with a spade-shaped beard.

'Still she's as good as gold,' Harry said. 'Here in the shop she never once transgressed.'

'House trained you might say,' said the man with the gold teeth.

'Nothing amiss with dung in its own place,' said the

66

farmer.

Harry's professional coat had once, but a long time ago, been white. He was shaving the man with the gold teeth and trimming the farmer, and he moved between them like a man who couldn't make up his mind which was which. Now and again he paused before a spotty mirror, and pulled and pushed at the mottled skin of his face and studied his bloodshot eyes. His hand was shaking very badly.

'It's a godsend,' he said, 'to have your own cow when you have a lot of children.'

A battered radio, fixed to the wall above the mirror, allowed a human voice, punctuated by atmospheric explosions, to sing about Genevieve, sweet Genevieve.

'The old girl's still threshing,' said the man with the gold teeth. 'Last heard her name mentioned in Boston.'

He made himself comfortable in the chair while Harry absented himself for a moment to snip at the farmer. He crossed his long legs. He had huge feet and shiny patent leather boots which he surveyed with interest.

'It riles me,' he said. 'Young folk around here have no enterprise. Market day now, go-ahead young fellow could take a fortune out there on the High Street. As a shoeshine.'

'He'd have to kneel down,' said the farmer.

Quoting from a patriotic ballad I'd learned at school, in which a brave blacksmith refused to stoop to shoe the horse of a redcoat captain, Harry said, 'I kneel but to my God above, I ne'er will bow to you.'

'People in this town,' said the farmer, 'find it hard enough to kneel to the Creator that made them, let alone to clean another man's shoes. Towney pride.'

'Pride never pockets dollars,' said the man from Boston.

Inexplicably the volume of the radio rose like a tidal wave and the talk was drowned in one last despairing wail to Genevieve.

'Switch her off,' said the Boston man. 'Get her outa here.'

'More likely,' said Harry as he evicted Genevieve, 'the mean mountainy farmers would spit on you or walk over you if you were misguided enough to kneel down to clean the cowdung off their boots.'

'No harm in cowdung,' said the farmer, 'in its proper

place.'

'Country's not organized,' said Gold Teeth. 'No co-operation.'

They went on like that while, unnoticed, I sat in trepidation and foreboding of the moment when the two would leave and I would be alone with, and at the mercy of, Harry.

The old farmer was the first to go. He stood up stiffly and Harry handed him a black bowler and a blackthorn stick. He wore nailed boots and leather leggings. When he took out a cloth purse to pay, as he put it, for the shearing, he turned his back on the company while he opened it and extracted the coins. But he gave me a penny as he passed and a pat on the head. The Boston man was better still. He mopped his face for a long time with a hot damp towel, and swayed like a feinting boxer before the mirror, and dried his face with another towel, and tossed a wide-brimmed straw hat in the air, and caught it on his head as it was descending, and shook hands with Harry and pretended to box him, and spun a half-crown at me, and shook my hand when I fielded it and was gone with a slam of the door that set the bell jangling for ages. Rich I was then beyond the dreams of avarice, but I needed it all as divine compensation for what was to follow.

'Kneel up on the chair, lad,' said Harry, 'or my back will be broke stooping to you.'

Brightly I began to recite, 'I kneel but to my God above ...'

'The cleverness of some people,' said Harry. 'But kneel up all the same.'

So up I knelt, my back to the mirror, my face to a wall papered with coloured illustrations of running horses, and Harry the High Priest robed me in a sacrificial cloth that like his coat of office had been white a long time ago. From faraway pastures the diminutive cowherd returned, ash twig in hand, and stood boldly staring at my misery; only then, as I looked at the little round marble of a close-cropped head, and as the scissors began to snip around my ears, did I realize with sickening horror what was in store for me. Doomed I was to receive one of the first crewcuts ever administered in our town — outside Harry's own family, that is, or the fever hospital where they cropped the heads of the scarlatina patients.

That negative hairstyle has since then become for a while one of the fashionable things but, at that period and in that town, it was a disgrace and humiliation. To be balded was a rural disorder, to be an object of laughter like the country boys who came with their parents into the town for market days and holidays of obligation. To be balded was an uncouth and backward way to be; and to make things worse, once already in my life I had, through an excess of masculine vanity, brought that disgrace and humiliation on myself. The relentless scissors snipped. The hideous little herd eyed me. Swathed in off-white garments I was powerless to escape. Behind tightly shut eyelids I saw my aunt's long, thatched, whitewashed farmhouse, ten miles from the town. Every summer I holidayed there. There was a great farmyard with barns, byres and stables, a deep orchard, and stepping-stones across the bog-red water of the burn that went down to join the Fairywater. There was a vile-tasting duck-pond that I once fell into, cherry trees that were regularly spoliated by the blackbirds and by bare-footed boys passing the road to school; and my dowager of an Aunt Kate peering through spectacles on the tip of her nose at the eggs she polished for market.

There was also Cousin Patrick's enviable jungle of glossy, curling, black hair.

'Aunt Kate,' my query would go, 'how can I make my hair curl like Patrick's?'

She was a tall, aged, angular widow, clad in black bombazine with beads on the bosom; and buttoned boots; and skirts to her ankles. Polishing eggs and peering she would answer absently: Patrick was forever and always out in the rain. It was the rain made his hair curl.

So every shower, soft or heavy, that blew up that summer from the south-west, found me standing under it as patient as the stump of a bush. The wagtails, for whom the rain brought up the worm and the white grubs, picked and hopped around me like mechanical toys. I became their friend and familiar. The way to catch wagtails, I was told, was to put salt on their tails and then catch them, but that summer I felt that I could without salt have captured the full of an aviary. We were rain-worshippers together. But when, in the middle of a downpour that came to cool earth and air after thunder and lightning, I was found, soaked to the skin and standing under a sycamore to get the added hair-curling benefit of the drops from the sodden leaves, Aunt Kate altered her advice.

'Once,' she said, 'Patrick had his hair cut very short and it was curly when it grew again.'

She was too old and too gentle, and too interested in polishing eggs, to allow for the ruthless literalness and pure faith of childhood, or to foresee the self-shearing I was to do with her best scissors out behind the red-currant bushes in the most secluded corner of the orchard. The roars of laughter with which the servant-boys around the farm greeted me convinced me that a shorn head was a shameful thing, and that I had accepted too readily the casual words of a rambling old woman; and a balded head became forever the mark of a fool. But then it didn't matter so much in the country where bald-headed little boys were the fashion and where there was nobody of much importance to see you. By the time the holidays were over my luxuriant locks had almost grown again — as uncurled as ever.

But this was far and away worse. The barber's baleful little son stared at me without speaking and then, unfeelingly, began to munch a crab-apple. Harry was a shaking, red-faced, savage Apache, and I knew I was being scalped. Between me and the shelter of home and my school cap there were leagues of crowded streets where everybody knew me, and on the day after tomorrow, the fabulous city of Dublin where there was no such thing as a baldy boy, and where thousands of people would stop on the street to look and laugh at the wonder.

Like a terrified mouse I ran all the way home, taking no time even to buy sweets with my hoard of money. Only it would further have drawn attention to my nakedness, I would have tried to hide my shaven crown with my hands. One corner-boy, perceiving my plight, called, 'Wee scaldy-bird, did you fall out of the nest?'

The memory of featherless baby birds, once seen in a nest, afflicted me with nausea.

'He cut you a bit close,' my mother said placidly. 'But it'll grow again.'

Putting on my school cap firmly I went out to the garden at the back of the house and sat on a stone and just looked at the ground.

The journey was a glory. The world stayed there, swimming in sunshine while I swept past like a king or an angel and inspected it from on high. It gave me my first vision of the Mountains of Pomeroy, as the song calls them, which aren't mountains at all but green, smooth, glacial hills; and the apple orchards of Armagh; and the slow-flowing sullen River Bann; and the great valley around the town of Newry; and the Mountains of Mourne, which are real mountains, sweeping down to the sea as they do in another song; and the Irish Sea itself, asleep along the flat shores of Louth and Meath and North County Dublin, or creeping on hands and knees into estuaries and the harbours of little towns. I sucked hard sweets and kept my eyes to the window and didn't have to expose myself by taking off my head-covering. My father told me the name of everything, and once when a hapless fellow townsman, who was travelling in the same carriage, made a fool of himself by mistaking the Mourne Mountains for the Hills of Donegal, my father silenced him with a genial glance and the words, 'Weak on topography, James.'

'I never travelled like you, Tommy,' the sad man said apologetically. 'I never saw Africa nor the Barbadoes.'

Being at the age when a boy thinks his father knows everything — before he grows a little older and comes to think, with equal foolishness, that his father knows nothing — I was mightily pleased, and so was my father who prided himself on his knowledge of places.

So, two happy men, we came to the station at Dublin and stepped out onto the interminable platform, and I took three steps and knew I was doomed. It was bad enough to be a leper, but it was torture out and out to have to carry a bell to draw public attention to your misfortune. Those three steps on the hard platform told me that, as fatally as any leper, I bore with me my self-accusing bell. It went clink-

clink-clink. It was the iron tip on the heel on my left shoe. For days it had been threatening to come loose and jingle and this, in the sorry malevolence of things, was the moment it would choose. Clink, clink, clink. To me it was as audible as the clanking chains of an ancestral ghost. The irritating sound came up distinctly over the puffing and shunting of engines, the shouting of porters, the rattling of their barrows. It went to hell altogether as I hobbled, trying to be inconspicuous, down the marble steps to the street, and was still audible above the sound of trams and buses, motor cars and four-wheeled horse drays. To the farthest limits of the city I heard it proclaim the arrival of that wonder of wonders, the Celebrated Bald Boy who was ashamed to take off his cap. All around me moved thousands of smooth-spoken, elegantly dressed, hatless, capless, velvet-footed people with heads of hair to be proud of. No city person would be barbarous enough to have iron tips on the heels of his or her boots or shoes. They didn't seem to notice me as I passed, but I imputed that to their excessive politeness. Behind unsmiling masks of faces they were really paralytic with mocking laughter. To look back I didn't dare in case I'd see somebody staring in hilarious wonder after my clinking retreat.

'The zoo I promised you,' my father said. 'The zoo you must have. We'll have the convent afterwards for a change. You're rattling like all the hammers in Hamilton's smithy.'

That recall to the homely image of the three good giants and their workshop fortified me for the walk to the restaurant for lunch. Keeping my eyes steadfastly down, and priding myself on coming from a land where giant men could swing hammers as city people couldn't, I resolved to see only the feet of the passing people and, after a while, I found myself repeating to myself, as if the words had magic and amusement in them: Feet, feet, feet, big feet, little feet, clean feet, dirty feet, and so on. For there were all sorts of feet in the world and, lacking feet, walking was not possible, and thinking of feet took my mind away from heads. The restaurant posed no new trials. Undisturbed, my heel didn't rattle. It was the day of a big hurling match and the place was full of red-faced countrymen who ate with their caps on. Their example was good enough for me and, eating my food,

72

I told myself with heavenly glee that within an hour I would, for the first time in my life, see elephants and monkeys, lions, tigers, cobras, kangaroos, all the wonders of swamp, savannah and jungle.

But, alas, even my time in the zoo was torn and agonized by changing, conflicting emotions. Most of the caged animals, like the red-faced countrymen with their caps on, seemed to be my allies. There was a lot of baldness among them, particularly on the most unexpected parts of the monkeys. The brown orang-outang, swinging round and round on a pole and apparently content to do just that for the whole long day, didn't appear to be in the least worried by his bald patches. But was the pitiful, pacing restlessness of the spotted hyena the result of some clumsy jungle barber stumping his tail — possibly with snapping teeth? The long grey-white hair of the lazy, peaceful llama; and hair like a crown on the top of the hump of the white Arabian dromedary; the legs of the polar bear that were so hairy they made him look as if he were wearing white pyjamas far too big for him; the mane of the King of beasts that no drunken barber would ever defile — all these convinced me that hair was immortal and resilient and would, except in the case of the crowns of old men, grow again. But then the hairless, slinking creatures filled me with horror: pythons, crocodiles, alligators, terrapins, turtles, monitor lizards with forked darting tongues, even the enormous hippo wallowing in muddy water and turning his unmannerly tail-end to all visitors. The sea-lion was redeemed by his antics and his whiskers.

The lovely little hairy toy-ponies from Shetland pulled charabancs crowded with laughing children and clinked their harness bells so as to drown the noise of my loose heel-tip. Every time they swept past, my father said, 'Care for a jaunt, boy?'

To the point of tears I refused, for my heart was bursting to board one of those charabancs. But how could I explain that I was afraid and ashamed in case some boisterous city boy among the passengers might knock off my cap and expose me to mockery?

A great eagle, motionless and alone in pride on a tree in a high wired enclosure, looked as if he was even proud of his bald head. But other birds, I thought, leave him solitary up there just because he is bald; and his grim, stern, isolated image haunted me all across the city to the gate of the convent, the Nazareth House, where my cousin, Sister Barbara, was a nun and where my greatest agony was to begin. Looking, with my cap on me, at captive animals, was one thing. Being looked at, when my cap was off, was another and nuns and orphans are awful people for looking at you.

'Call everybody sister,' said my father, 'except the reverend mother and, when I find out which of them she is, I'll give you a dig in the ribs. And take your cap off, I'm sorry to say,' said he. 'We have to act like gentlemen and nuns are ladies.'

He pressed the convent bell. The gate slowly opened and we looked into a whole cosmos of giggling girls in blue dresses and white bows and pigtails and shiny shoes. Oh my misfortune and unholy luck that it should have been playtime for all the little female orphans in the convent just when I arrived among them looking more like an orphan than any one of them. They didn't, I suppose, see many boys, and a bald-headed boy, his face purple with blushing, his cap in his hand, his heel-tip rattling, was just too good to be true. Looking back at it now I can, perhaps, admit that those little atomies of womanhood giggled every day and all the time, at playtime. But at that moment, when the door-portress, all swinging rosary beads and flapping black tails, led us across the playground, I felt that every giggle was meant for me, and I cursed Harry the Barber to places Dante never heard of and hoped that overnight his red cow with the crumpled horn would change into a slinking, odorous, odious hyena; or into a pacing tiger that would devour his cowherd of a son; or that all his customers would change into reptiles condemned to wander sleek and hairless to the judgment seat of God and beyond.

A door closed behind us. The giggles were no longer heard. We followed the portress along a passage polished with such extravagance that it must have cost many a visitor, or hapless convent chaplain, a broken femur or radius. Into a parlour with a bare polished table in the centre of the floor, twelve stiff chairs around, and a portrait on the wall of a man that my father said was an archbishop. Nobody, you were sure, had ever lived or laughed in that room. The door closed behind the departing portress. The archbishop frowned down at us.

'Your heel in the passage,' said my father, 'would outsound the convent bells.'

With the shame burned into me by the giggles I hadn't for a while heard the heel. I had been the fox who lost his brush, the Chinese mandarin who lost his pigtail.

'Put your hoof on this chair here to see if I can do anything about it.'

He pulled and hammered, and stopped pulling because he said if the heel-tip came the shoe would come with it and, possibly, the foot as well. He was still hammering, hoping for the best, when the door opened and six nuns entered, including the reverend mother and, bringing up the tail of the procession, two lay-sisters bearing food for the two of us. What they saw was a perspiring middle-aged man beating with the black bone handle of the big claspknife with which he cut his tobacco at the heel of the shoe of a bald little boy.

With what composure he could muster my father greeted them, introduced his heir, and the two of us sat down to eat and the five nuns and the reverend mother sat down in a semi-circle to look at us. That's the way you eat when you go to a convent. This was the zoo and my father and myself were the nut-cracking monkeys. There was talk, too, of course, and Sister Barbara gave us each an envelope full of holy medals and leaflets. But at no moment would I have been surprised if reverend mother had tossed me a nut and, obeying instinct, I had fielded, shelled and eaten it all in one sweeping gesture, as but lately I had seen the black baboon do.

When the eating was over the reverend mother said, 'Now your little boy, I feel sure, can sing.'

She might also have said: Your little boy can, I feel sure, by the cut of him and the head of him, swing round a pole like a orang-outang.

The way it was I might as well have been singing as sitting there, so up I stood and breathed deeply and squared myself

75

for action. If I had had hair on my head I wouldn't have lost my wits and would, like any Christian gentleman, have sung about Erin remembering the days of old ere her faithless sons betrayed her. As it was, with the strain and the shame, and with the naked soft top of my head exposed to the raging elements, I went mad and sang a song I had heard sung when the Hamiltons swung their mighty hammers above the burning iron.

'One Paddy Doyle,' I told the nuns, 'lived in Killarney and he loved a maid named Betsy Toole.'

It went on from bad to worse, but when my mortified parent made a move to stop me the reverend mother raised her hand and said, 'It was my father's favourite song — Doran's Ass.'

'Now Paddy that day had taken liquor,' I assured them, 'which made his spirits feel light and gay. Says he, the devil a bit use in walking quicker for I know she'll meet me on the way.'

The shrill playing voices of the giggling girls were faraway as I related how drunken Paddy fell asleep in the ditch with Doran's jackass and embraced the animal in mistake for his true love. My voice was a bawdy bleat in the hollow, holy heart of eternity.

When the song had ended and I had modestly accepted the applause there was more talk and the lay-sisters brought in ice-cream. Then the reverend mother and Sister Barbara walked us across a playground now mercifully empty and bade farewell at the gate. The reverend mother put her hand into a slit in the side of her habit and went down and down until the better half of her arm vanished, then surfaced again with a box of chocolates in the hand. She gave it to me, and stooped and kissed the tonsured crown of my head.

'That song,' she said, 'I haven't heard it in years.'

'That I could easily believe,' said my father as the gate closed behind us.

Then in awed tones he added, 'There's no doubt about it. Suffer the little children. Come on, son, and we'll see the laughing mirrors in the Fun Palace before we catch the rattler.'

The box of chocolates shone like a sun.

'Haven't nuns, da,' I said, 'terrible deep trouser pockets?'

So perturbed I was and yet, because of the chocolates, so overjoyed that I was in the tram on my way to the centre of the city before I realized I had left my cap in the convent parlour.

'Leave it be,' said my father. 'They can have it as a relic of the man who told them about Paddy Doyle and Doran's Ass. Their prayers and that kiss of peace will make your golden locks grow again as strong as corn stubble.'

In the Fun Palace there were two girls in bathing suits lying in cubes of ice to show they could do it, and a fat woman who weighed forty stone and wore an outsize bathing suit and who looked at me and slapped her thigh and laughed and said to my father, 'Ain't I a dainty little lass?'

In this underground world the Celebrated Bald Boy could fade into his background and be a freak among freaks.

In a glass case a witch with a conical hat raised both hands when sixpence went into a slot and a printed slip telling your fortune came out of another slot. In another glass case a ghost, obligingly, and also for sixpence entered a sombre panelled room and frightened a man in a four-poster bed so that he hid under the bedclothes. The ghost, having done his sixpennyworth of haunting, vanished backways through a crack in the panelling.

Ardent queues lined up to peer into a small lighted glass box to share the butler's keyhole vision.

'It wouldn't interest us,' my father said.

He steered me past the devotees and we paid our money and stepped into the hall of mirrors which, at first sight, might have been the hall of maniacs, because the six or seven people within were looking at the walls and doubling up and roaring with laughter. So I turned and looked into the first mirror and saw my father, twelve feet long if he was an inch, and wriggling like the eel I once saw in semi-sunlit water under the arch of Donnelly's bridge on the Camowen river. Standing beside him as I was, I was yet, in the most uncanny fashion, completely invisible; and in the second mirror my father was a little fat schoolboy and my bald head was a Shrove Tuesday pancake with currants for eyes; and in the third mirror my father was all head and no body and I was all legs topped by a head like a pine cone. By the fourth mirror the tears of laughter were blinding me and, in blurred vision, I saw red-faced Harry shaking like an aspen leaf; and the man from Boston, all gold teeth, jumping and dancing and swinging from the farmer's beard; and the reverend mother with an arm a mile long pulling boxes of chocolates out of a bottomless pocket; and the red cow with sloppy feet slithering and sitting down in Harry's shop and refusing to get up; and the giant Hamiltons, adopting all shapes and sizes, and confronted with hammers either so tiny as to be useless or too big and heavy to raise off the ground. The whole world I knew and the people in it were subject to comic mutation.

'Stop laughing, son,' said my father at last, 'or we'll miss the train.'

He wiped the tears from my eyes but he mightn't have bothered. They were as wet as ever before I got to the street. Every man and woman I looked at could have been cavorting before a comic, distorting mirror. There was something laughably odd about every one of them: big noses, red faces, legs too long or too short, behinds that waggled, clothes that didn't fit. Every one of them had a cow in the house. My bald head mattered no longer: it cut me off from no community. Let whoever liked laugh at me, I'd laugh back.

Tramping up the long platform I realized that a great silence had come around us. Engines snorted and shunted, trucks rattled, porters called each other names, newsboys sang their wares in sounds that weren't real words, fat women panicked and began to gallop in case the train might elude them. Yet, lacking one sound, it was all silence, and there was no clink-clink-clink, no warning note of my leper bell. Somewhere between the laughing mirrors and the station the iron tip had parted company with the heel and left me to walk as catfooted as an Aran islander or a wild Indian in pampooties, while it lay lost and neglected forever to be rolled over or walked on by the city's traffic. A part of me and of my town had died in exile and sorrow touched me for a while. Had I only detected the moment of our parting I could have preserved the heel-tip as a keepsake — warm in my trousers' pocket.

But it was no evening for enduring sorrow. Before me lay the sights and thrills of the journey, and the reverend mother's chocolates, and the joys of telling and retelling, and expanding for colour and poetry, my traveller's tales. In the schoolroom again when the shiny round ball that was the world was set spinning I knew I could follow it for more than a hundred miles and tell my compeers that convents in the city were stuffed full of boxes of chocolates to reward brave boys who could sing; that, while China might be busting with Chinamen, there were, in a house on the quays by the Liffey, mirrors that turned all men into objects of laughter; and that, while Harry the barber might keep a cow in the house, it was little to what they kept closed in cages in the Phoenix Park in Dublin.

Arrival

EDWARD BRAZIL

Happy flight-heart begins evaporating after touchdown.
I arrive here with the memory of a Rothman's ad on an old
television set, the household god of suburbia. Of jets purring
on the runways of Schiphol and, supposedly, the greatest
duty-free zone on earth. Could purchase a car or a mink coat
but nobody to drive nor no one to wear. My romantic soul
starting to tatter, flakes falling off it not at all like the
holy bread but rather stale crisps, brown scabs. Life's axle
wears us bald, scarcely roadworthy as we skid, wobble, fall.
I realize this now though not wishing to.

And the farewells back in Dublin before departure. Parents
in summer gear, slightly tanned. See the museums, go
boating, write a postcard. Yes, yes. And Foley, who'd been
silent on the way out from the city, uneasy hush in the car as
we drove through Drumcondra, Whitehall and on to the main
road. He pulled me aside in the foyer, face like a tired
balloon on a scraggy Christmas tree. 'Listen, lad. Dip your
wick in a Dutch princess, else get ye to Germany where the
broads have big breasts.' Of course, of course.

My mother waved a hand at a Caledonian silver bird,
thinking I was on it. No, mother. To the right a little. Shiver
that paw at the bar where I'm sprouting my own wings on
the cheapest vodka in ages. Fear of leaving, fear of flying,
fear of reaching destination.

Now they are all an hour behind, a matter of channel and
land, especially around the English coast, cloudless, where
the sun struck and men were cigarette ash blown about in
brown and yellow saucers hemmed in, not by hedgerows
where birds nest, but by a neat scheme of chocolate biscuits,
suddenly free of their golden packets.

And as we wheeled over cityscape, in spite of seat belts
fastened, the feeling of being like a loosened feather on
a hawk's wing.

But, dear folks, I am here, arrived. And there is no castle with a portcullis through which I might peep at the ladies in the courtyard unhitching their stays for the pleasure of the King who wolfs wild fowl, waiting. No, nor a fairground with nimble little girls looking for ribbons. Ribbons for love (I'll buy one or two), love for ribbons (three or four).

Not even, mirabile dictu, a promise of tulips.

Foley, you've sent me to a larger Dublin, international snake-pit, its people concealing a deadly bile in their throats. Thanks, fiend-friend. It was nice of you to think me nice and able. I will bring you back a windmill and a slip of Dutch lace for dreaming on.

By Grand Central Station I Sat Down And Wept. Elizabeth Smart, you were not pulling my leg, though yours was another time and country. But I have no time for women's rhetoric, no time. By Grand Central Station I gather up my rucksack and head off, feinting deftly twice a second so as not to be flattened by the electric trams eeling along centre-street, ringing, jiving, in tune to some secret music only the air can whisper. Steel ballerina-queens.

Down on the bank of a canal hippy-types loll about in the shade. There's smoke skirling up out of little fires over which cans of beans are balanced gingerly on pronged sticks. I watch from a height, overseer of primeval idiots.

Still, I think in my innocence that if I were to go down there, go down among God's own, I might spot the ghosts of Kerouac, Cassady (making sweet time with the willing ones) or maybe even big, lonely, sad Dave Kammerer whom the Greek boy stabbed. My naïveté is pure, but fathomless.

For I can only see youngsters armed with books (Tolkien and/or Hesse) trying to be hip intellectuals while all the time they're watching others for a response to their magnificence who in turn are watching them for the same thing. And neither party is offering anything. Ah, as the maths teacher said, the implications of the permutations of one-to-one-correspondence. The right shoe wanting to partner the left.

There are two people on the grass making love who are letting on to be wrestling. I study their efforts though it upsets me. I have come here myself to meet a match, to catch a young girl, preferably Dutch, the ones who giggle all the time and who, when asked 'You speak English?', reply with appropriate gesture of thumb and index finger 'Only a liddle.' Proceeding then to give you the King's English till your ears smart. Oh girls!

On down further so towards the city centre, past fruit stalls where the plums are peaches, the peaches melons, the melons . . . And the vendors are jolly over the unbeatable fruit. No Moore Street magicians here who can sneak two bad apples into a bag of six while you firmly believe you're walking away with a half dozen beauties.

On and on, past the wops selling multicoloured ices out of fridges mounted on bicycles. And a herd of Yanks, shuffling and snorting like wild buffalo, in line for a trip on a cruiser. Out on the canals, the boats themselves, streamlined and flash, are fizzing through the waters, ghost-gracefully and quiet as the swans who once disturbed the mirror under Leeson Street Bridge and turned my face all awry.

I finally reach the square and a belief that music is surely the happiest, most generous of the arts. Two guitarists, rusty Spanish-skinned, are running their fingers along the frets, loose and sure as the feet of ice-skaters. Heads list like shook corn, everyone singing, tapping, with faces doing what they were made to do, smile. Ah, yes! Sociability and mouthfuls of teeth. There is a woman in shadow at a window of the Palace. I wonder if she's royalty, royalty wishing she weren't, wanting to step down among the pigeons and go crazily dancing on the stones. I like to think she is, that she's not just a gawking servant, stealing some seconds away from polishing cutlery.

I walk on and go to the left whereas I should have kept to the right, but I'm quickly warming to the notion of pleasureable lostness among cafés and bars that hurl out jukebox jazz to rattle in the streets. I'm wondering where my girl is and whether she will be Dutch or German. Is that her there, sitting on a wooden stool, glass of beer in her hand, long cigarette in mouth, her silver-Cinderella slippers now become a pair of unwinged sandals? Or is she in the park over at the far side of the city, eyes like scuffed buttons, drugged, wondering should she join the queue for a VD check or not? Perhaps. But again, she may be out on the coast, hitching a lift in towards this place. We will meet in a day's time then, we will, we will.

'You like? You like?' Words tinkle nearby, but surely not for me. I look straight ahead, hangdog, shoulder-straps beginning to pinch.

'You like? You like?' A hand on my shoulder, feather-frail and white-glowing. I turn around. Black-booted, brown-thighed, pink-bloused shape on which a cute face squats. Blonde baby with two big chunky . . . earrings. God!

I blush, smirk, look around once more. No doubt about it. I'm being addressed, invited, sized up sexually and, of course, financially. The Palace clock rings six bells and I'm sweating despite myself, sticky fingers rooting in the fluff of my pockets. My rucksack is actually a hunch and I'm an old cherry-nosed man with a dirty mind, poring over pictures in an attic room.

'How much, love?' I recover equanimity, embrace bravado, my mind a ready-reckoner, assured of the inclination, just waiting for the price.

'For you, fifty guilders.' Speaking, she sent her hands a-ripple on her hips, tossed her long hair.

Fifty guilders. Seven pounds. Cheap or dear? I cannot say for definite, having no previous dealings with which to compare, only rumours and false pride of friends. Foley who got one in March on Mount Street for four quid — an auburn wild-cat, never satisfied, who 'tore away like a tinker's shirt' and to whom he'd given a tip of twenty pence — later calling me from my sleep to gloat over my virginity like a millionaire kicking a sixpence aside on the pavement. And then O'Connor who decided to take French lessons in Soho, genuinely intending to master the language with a girl named Françoise (what else?) but who left the conditional and past tenses behind after an evening of soixante-neuf. What am I to do now, friends? Fifty guilders. Seven pounds. Cheap or dear? Might not be clean. Might knock off my traveller's cheques while kissing. Might not live up to expectations. Forgive me, mother. Don't chide me, father. Bless me, Father, for I have sinned. How my child and how often? An old man through the grating, eager to listen and absolve by a babble of Latin.

'No thanks, love. Some other time.'

I am upset because she is not upset by my refusal. Passion and desire collapse. Hustlers consider love as it is, a frozen fish, cold-eyed, arctic.

We separate, my steps hurting me, a distance growing and distaste keeping pace with it for I know, without looking, that she's gliding towards another. Who? A novice hiker like myself, covetous of love yet brilliant with fear? Or an old banker, free for the evening from his hotel suite and a wife with toothache, out on the pretext of a letter to be posted, his limbs to be exercised, by a walk of course?

Oh supple mare, don't go, don't go. I'd like to take you to a field, put the moon on your shoulder, lie in the ferns and wake with our eyes at the morning.

She is gone now. I fish out map and pencil from my pocket, take my bearings. This city's arranged like a spider's web on which I mark myself down darkly, a fly at the mercy of spiders yet to be encountered. Along streets becoming hushed, I move on back to the square, empty now, the music a memory, a man hosing the cobble stones beneath the Palace where the royalty must surely be listening to after-dinner voice of poet, tinkle of violin.

And so on over bridges, the canals whispering, turning mildly like dark conger eels. Innumerable boats on them, clumping with a weary resonance. There is a little doorway, quaint, beneath a sign and I expect a merchant to emerge at any moment, dressed à la Renaissance, who is going to ask me if I've ever been to Florence or heard the name 'de Medici'.

I buy a postcard before reaching the sleep-in. I take a goodnight look at the city. She is painting her face, opening the clasp of her jewellery box to a wonder of brightness, beads to rest against the skin of her neon neck, the night-life trove that beckons money out of pockets.

I push open a door and amble inside for my night's rest, pick a path through the many big 650 c.c. motorbikes with German number plates, low familiar croon of Dylan curling out from some hidden stereo and, as I pay for a berth and get my wrist stamped blue by an attendant, I find myself singing 'Percy's Song' along with the voice that comes at me from all different angles. I hand over my rucksack and receive a pink ticket in return. The nose of the cloakroom girl is saddled with freckles but she looks fine in a suit of cords. Then I move away from the hatch, a hundred eyes on me walking, burning little piss-holes in my mind.

The warehouse resembles a Victorian den: to the left, Fagin and entourage are plotting the perfect robbery; to the right, Swinburne & Co. pervert themselves in a corner. I must conceal bewilderment, seem unimpressed, not raw, fresh, green, haul back my eyes from off their sticks. But it's a difficult business.

There are young people on the floor, on couches, on counters, on each other, smoking from pipes which they hand on to the ones beside them, big with the notion of sharing and being part of the round. Old Gaeltacht peasants minus turf-fire, St Patrick and fifty-odd years, getting merrily stoned on Pakistani, etc.

Through swinging door with a cold beer in my fist, I reach the sleeping quarters, room of a thousand bunk-beds on which kids are sleeping, smoking, drinking, gambling, goof-balling and loving openly.

In the wash room, a girl (definitely a Swede because of that desirable North European tang that unfurls off her like scent of grass or timber, newly cut) steps naked from behind a curtain, Venus from the baths, milky, wet-skinned and eminently the essence of everything that matters. She catches my greedy stare, smiles and patters past. The beer halts in my throat, comes back up to my mouth like sour stuff. Before she disappears, she swings around, faces me, giggles and kicks her leg up like a Tiller girl. Ah, ma coquette, I will not smile at this for it's so much the Irish ploy of tease, be followed and refuse. And I like to think these tricks left well behind at a safe geographical distance; I should not have to watch them here performed by much finer women.

I walk outside to pick my bed for the night, some top bunk preferably, close to the safety of gable or corner walls. I find a good spot, lie down on my sleeping bag on my side so that I can watch the comings and goings through the far doors. Each time they are pushed apart I can hear music from the outer room with which I sing along even after the shut doors have locked away all traces of the tunes. Sometimes I sing so perfectly that when the doors are ajar for more than once during the same song, I can preserve the rhythms and pace of the singers when I am left to do my own little turn in the silence. It's not much but it comforts.

Across the way, a pair are sleeping, the boy's hand rests on the girl's breast and she wears a huge smile as though an actual pose of boy and girl lying close like that has just shot by her, an image from one of her sweeter dreams. Beyond them, a drugged kid is tracing invisible pictures in the air with her thumbs, expressions of delight and wonderment on her face as she sketches.

To my right, incongruously, an old man clutching a canvas bag lies back tiredly on his coat as though some ghostly nurse were setting him gently down in a bed of newest linen.

Before I fall asleep, I prop myself up to write the postcard, a glossy photo of a hurdy-gurdy man, laughing beside his machine on Rosengracht. 'Dear Mam and Dad. Arrived safely. Weather O.K. This is a great city. Have made some friends already. Love, Michael.'

I slip it under my pillow for posting in the morning.

Banished Misfortune

DERMOT HEALY

The house that Saul lived in.

While the children slept there, outside it rained. The whole night long. Though it was warm and brown among the damp shiny chestnuts, the weather had opened under the shadows of the rambling trees. Everything was falling. The thump of chestnuts on the soft floor of the night. And the insects thrived down there in the caves of leaves. Eileen slept facing east, young child limbs learning to fly and the people of Belfast looking up in wonder. The duchess hopped along the stairs, past the dusty quiet of McFarland's door where the mother turned often in her sleep down an empty and alien past, and the cat sat up beside the small steamy window with the lead stripes to catch her breath, where the magpies had chewed the new putty. Listening to the water swirling over the stones and the loose gate banging in the lower meadow. And when little Tom coaxed her down onto the bed, she put her washing away and jumped like a little deer.

– Here puss, he said and she stretched out one long paw.

For whatever reason the house might fall, the sleeping McFarland would build again with a sense of adventure anywhere north of the lakes and in good time, son of Saul, master builder of Fermanagh county but by pneumonia put away while tended by his wife Olive, Glan woman and descendant of J. O'Reilly who danced once with flax in his trousers, and though nominally christian died in foreign and pagan lands fighting an unjust war, but McFarland sensing the lie of the land grew away from a sense of guilt or desire for power and prayed that the haphazard world would not destroy his family so well grounded among the moralities of chance and nature, if one could remain loyal to the nature of a people and not the people themselves, for whatever reason the house might fall.

The door opened onto the fields.

All round, that silence and damp air of expectancy after the eerie rasp of the storm had blown over.

Judy, his wife, cooked over a single gas jet in the leafy half light for the electricity black-out was at its worst and it seemed to McFarland like one of those early mornings years ago when he had risen in the cold to feed the cattle and heard the groan of the house and Saul's asthmatic breathing overhead. Still the echo of the sessions that had gone on through the night when he was a child. The children put on two sets of jumpers and climbed into their boots under the stairs, and Eileen picked up a toy soldier knocked over by the foot of the father as he went round the back to examine the roof for missing slates. Soft Chinese music of the rain on glass and leaves, lightly touched cymbals, ducks crashing onto the waters, the primitive crane stretching her awkward wings in a lone high flight, the land below so cold and misty it looked as if a healing frost had settled.

Little Tom chased Eileen sideways through the mist to the end of the garden, among the penitent crumbling apple trees, in her new frock and washed hair and everywhere a silent promise that she might be well.

— The night it being dark in my favour, the father sung fretfully to himself in the boot of the car, unconcerned about the helicopter that flew over the house and scattered the birds that a moment before had been strolling along the hedges. Humming a reel like a dream he was trying to remember, McFarland, out of an incapacity to deal with the extravagance of small details, involved his wife and children in discovering the pattern from last year for fitting in the cases, instruments and bags. He scraped the fiddle bow thoughtfully under his chin and sang it backwards and forwards across his ear as he went through the mathematics. Talking in a holiday voice to nuts and screws and old newspapers, while his wife reasoned with the children, losing her patience. Will Byrne, the sentinel of the hill, his brother murdered at his door, watched their activities with benign speculation as he lay against an old railing from which he propelled himself every few seconds and took a quick low whistle, escaping from the past for a few excruciating moments.

88

— You get in the back with your mother, the father said and little Tom put the cat down reluctantly in the shed and dropped a chicken bone temptingly into her dish. She was sitting at a ladylike distance away, upset by the jamming of the doors and all those signs of departure. He hid another bigger bone behind the shed after whistling down the fields, watching a weasel drink water from the cup of a leaf among the chopped timber. The duchess suddenly attended to her wardrobe. The soft scuffle of leaves and harness. After they had all driven away, the dog, with pebbles hanging from his coat, came in mumbling because he had been forgotten and the cat flew up onto the rafters, while above her the rain slanted to the west.

— What'll we sing, asked little Tom.

The father looked up to heaven, his musical children vain and happy by turns, his child wife looking steadfastly silently ahead as she always did when they journeyed together, always heading off into some fitful future, living off the excitement of leaving something intangible behind and the wheels on the road had a life of their own. Edging down the lane, the dark purple of the sloes, sour grapes, the black-berries tidily hung between the bronze leaves and yellow roots of the hedge. Lakes, a darker purple than the sloes away below the chestnut trees. A soldier's jeep was parked on the crossroads, guns cocked. 'You can learn to live with anyone,' Saul had said, 'it's imperial to me!' And McFarland, reared amongst a series of foreign and local escapades, took everywhere his copies of the Arctic and Antarctic voyages. 'Irish musicians are a crowd of drunken children,' Judy said to him once as they drank Guinness from a bedroom sill in a boarding-house. 'I suppose it wasn't what the Lord wanted,' he said eventually, away from her down to the Roscommon men strolling through the riotous, melancholy music. Still, tucked under his elbow as he sauntered through the dark deserted streets of Belfast where the men drank gin and the women drank whiskey, he always had his copy of Scott's final trip up the frozen Pole, a book he had read many many times and still felt the same harsh ecstasy the explorers must have experienced when, worn to the bone of humanity, they discovered that the Norwegians had been there before them.

And the other explorers held down by the winter, frozen and breathless and singing songs under the snow.

The family drove through the clouds and Friday the dog chased round the farm for the scents that were fast fading.

Eileen lit the matches for her father's cigarettes, cupping her awkward hands like the men do in the yard to save the light from the wind. Like she was reading the future from the palms of her hands, stained with the juices of the early-morning leaves where so many faces and voices were hidden. And all round strange wet farmhouses, the finely cropped trees of the north, cut like mushrooms or birds settling with wings tucked, fine cars in the driveways along the wide fields, the distinctive roadway signs, the extinct lorries. Behind, the sheds like railway carriages and over the hills the grim Norse-like churches. Going over the bridges there was a great empty feeling beneath your heart as the car rose. Like a roof lifting off a house. Her mother's agitated face when their uncle threatened. If time could wait. Once Eileen's stomach turned sick, mesmerized by the sudden looseness of her limbs, her head swaying. McFarland walked her up and down a laneway off the main road with his tolerant musical strides, while overhead the trees joined branches in the mist that was blinding the islanders as they rowed ashore on the flooded Erne, adjusting to the repeated deaths beside the blue frosted lakes, at night the cool drinks, hands dexterous at cards. She hated these moments that she had no control over. But it was better to be sick and let her eyes film over with tears for a moment, than arrive bleary-eyed and fatigued after dosing herself with the heavy languorous pills she took as a child that made her memory falter. Her hair was cut so short for her face that she showed pain too easily. And she was irked by Tom's cheerfulness behind her in the car, her instincts left in him.

— A big girl like you won't find the time passing, his voice above her, afraid of any weakness that might handicap their security, humming and smoking in the mist with his hand on her shoulder, we'll be there in no time. 'We'll be there in no time,' he said.

And that's how little Tom, anxious to laugh, attracting laughter, succeeded in getting into the front seat beside his father to pull the window down and trail his hands near the low trees that flew by like the wind, too quick even for his eyes to catch, and wave at the Customs man as they crossed the last ramp and headed down the bad easy roads, the Leitrim-Cavan border where traditions had survived even the Famine itself, a roofless countryside without trees or soldiers or gunfire at night but the road through the frost-shattered mountains and stray rain-filled clouds, the bilberry bushes and cotton grass. And Sandy Byrne and Friday were leaping through hedges and streams on their way to the village after Old Byrne had cursed the skyline and chased them from his house with a broom. McFarland's eyes were fading, he grieved sometimes for them in the early morning when his vision was hazy like that shortness of breath, and now he was aware of Tom watching him squeeze his eyes, concentrate, slow down and take the centre of the road. After the humours of Ballyconnell they crossed the dry streams where the railway lines had been lifted and sold to the Congo by order of an ecumenical government, here several of his mother's people had flagged down a train and never been seen again, going away with a wisp of smoke and single words in the old Irish. Among the Chinese and gunpowder, among poets and moneygrabbers his grandfather had been there for the driving of the last spike on the Great Pacific Railway till he fell down a frozen thirty-foot falls, his dogs screaming in terror below him and all over the snowswept Canadian valley.

— Tisin' no wonder this is the wee county that Sean Maguire sprang from, the father said remembering, and thought of the boy in the gap and the lady's top dress and the day he had climbed here with Saul and had a nose-bleed on the mountain.

They left behind the pagan air of Glan, grey damp farms surrounded by cluttered rusty galvanized sheds, washing blowing in the garden, a pump on the road that nobody used, cottages with the thatch sunk in the middle. A huge aerial. The mother slept laxly, hearing Bach's Fantasy and Fugue on her husband's tape and she longed to lean out and draw someone close to her for a while, for someone, she said, tapped her on the shoulder naming various schoolchildren she had taught in Belfast, tall mousy-haired children who hardly ever talked or did in a rush and called to her house whispering angrily, and as her head bobbed against the rear seat she never saw her husband smile boyishly at her in the mirror. And Eileen copied her mother going to sleep, glancing through half-closed eyes at the blue-aproned women, sweeping, washing down their steps and the men crossing the streets with a multitude of different steps, their breath flying behind them. After the trip to Athlone the fiddle quietened, the bodhran settled, trees were down everywhere after the big wind. At various times they came across groups of men standing round with saws under their arms and greatcoats hung up on the side of a ditch. The mist was lifting like the curtain in the Town Hall. They saw the first house in Connaught. They heard the musical priest. And while the sky cleared the family ate next a stone wall, sharing the air with an odd horse that had been looking at the same spot in a gorse haggard for days. Thousands of sewage pipes were piled on the footpaths, a gate opened into a new lake. 'The bit of food,' Saul had said, 'it's like the man begging, it will take you to the next door.' And the Shannon had turned the streams into wild dancing streams, shucks filled with wild water that stranded the cows who wandered about ankle-deep in the muck searching for grass. At last, when they entered the city, a Friesian calf with a white star on his forehead and white back legs stopped the car in the middle of the road and peered in with large blinking enquiring eyes. 'A white-headed calf is very hard on the beast,' he'd said, 'turn him if you can, I'm the queer quack myself.'

Peace is not necessary here, she heard that and . . . these people would rather endure. Who was it? Was it him? And again. I think it was St Patrick started this campaign. Was it drunk together on the boat to Belfast, collecting stolen timber from his brother on the docks, his fat belligerent brother who could kill, or was it on another day not in a boat but crossing the road in hot weather when traffic was heavy? My young saintly maidenly unmarried sister sleeping with a Quaker in that deserted bullet-peppered block of flats, oh my sister how sometimes I miss your crusade for there's nothing left for me but to become a victim who at the end of all resources admits nothing.

    — Where are we now, the mother said, wakening.

    — Timbuktu, the boy said.

    — You so and so, the mother said, ruffling his hair.

    — I just combed that out a wee minute ago, said Eileen and she flicked out her own short hair, the holiday at last for real, trying to create some dancing curls, and patted down her fresh autumn dress and knocked the mud of the fields from her shoes, spread out her toes to release the sweet stiffness of the journey from her body, the stifling impression of having gone nowhere till she smelt the roots of the sea, the girl in her gliding down as Ennis slowed the pipes.

    Her father closing his eyes gratefully as he stopped the car.

    Slates littered the streets of Galway.

    Shopkeepers picked their way through the debris, gesticulating and looking up at the sky like sleepwalkers. The scene was obscenely familiar to the family from the north who felt for a moment slightly superior in their ability to deal with chaos, death, laughter at death. The family booked into a boarding house that looked out on a river that ran floundering under heavy stone bridges into the salmon sea, and the nervous landlady was filled with small talk about the storm, as a man held a ladder against the side of the building and his apprentice fought off cramp as he took a perilous path across the roof. The family listened with hidden humour to the stray southern accents, as men shouted encouragement to the climber from the street below. Little Tom mimicking. The boarding house began with a big room advancing in smaller rooms till it ended in a tiny toilet perched over the river. They spoke self-consciously of the weather and Judy glared at the son of the house who watched Eileen with cold mischievous lust as the girl stood downstairs at the discordant piano fingering the keys in time to the waves of the sea, that same rhythm in her hands as was in her eyes when they had sat in the deserted concert halls in Belfast and she was husbandless, to listen to the orchestra practising the songs of Fauré and the tiny early piano pieces of Mozart such a long time ago.

    And Friday had found the bone at the back of the shed

and took it down to the edge of the stream, where he drank
out of his own questioning reflection in the damp mossy
shadows where the hesitant rain and leaves still fell.

The slow earth.

— I'll be back early, said McFarland when everything was
settled and kisses had been handed round.

— God, oh God man, foolish promises, she answered him
and he smilingly pursed his lips and shook his shoulders and
with his fiddle case went down to a pub where the barman
was a retired monk and sung songs of Napoleon and Aquinas,
tapping and patting his companions down.

When first in Portaferry they crossed hands Eileen was
a small delighted baby, who had to travel each day by car
with her mother to school and the child never cried but lay
listless for hours in the nursery, only the high windows. And
when he and Judy married, the child tottered quietly into the
small church in autumn and laughed away brown-eyed at her
mother looking so serious. For those first few weeks Judy
tired easily of the endless sessions and retired early leaving
him alone among a bunch of new emptied musicianors. And
as the constant assault of songs and music wore away with his
first advances, and they learned each other's ways and the
way of the child, she was no longer like a false note in a slow
air returning and returning. She showed none of his cunning
reticence, was eager to slip into a thousand excitable
abstractions. Yet how many towns had they got so drunk in,
the world might end, playing squash in the early morning
handball alleys to soothe a hangover, her fine excited accent
a mixture of cynicism and distance. Because the city
restrained people, or so he believed, it would have been
customary for her sophistication to endure some rural
cynicism but in this instance it was his nature gave way,
slipping away into a thousand nearly familiar impressions.
The complexity attracted him, the adventure of a perfume
alien to his sheets, the lane to the door.

Cupping his man-root in her hand, old and awkward
gamblings, and she saying slow and he for all his mock
heroics learning for the first time the body's music, lightly
touched cymbals that rocked them both away.

Red berries next the house, and the sycamore releasing

a thousand revolving wings.

Judy brought the children for a long walk on the pier till evening caught them in an early long blue light like the sheen from a silk curtain and they strolled and ran back restlessly to the house. Not that Salthill was beautiful but ugly and plain and yet it was a necessary outing for them all although she was not certain that any of them might feel release, know the difference in such a short time for they had burrowed down so deep in anxiety that happiness was nearly hysterical. Little Tom's cheeks were warm and Eileen's hair had blown and blown in the wind and they were tired as kings now one day had ended. Judy had grown used to being on her own. In Belfast they had worked apart, she driving out of the city each morning to Lisburn to teach and he heading off in a blue van to some new disaster area. And after the sudden move to the old house and the death of the old man they were suddenly thrown into each other's company most of the day, like young lovers, finding themselves grown strange to each other as if their previous work had sustained some missing link, the whorls of wood now their guidelines, the sun striking the leafy paths under the bronze ashen trees. But one could not but feel relieved yet cowardly after being released from the rows of terraced houses. Back in their room with the wasting wallpaper and plastic flowers, the landlady's family downstairs watching the Saturday film on television, Tom turned bad-tempered and started to argue, pulling Eileen away from the ukulele she was playing. The invisible stars that blind each other. The boy started to hammer the bed with his fists and the girl squeezed her hands against her face screaming, while below the television was lowered.

— Stop. Stop, she screamed.
— Ya wanna see a wee bitch, he shouted.
— Leave me alone.
— Stop. Both of ye, yelled Judy.

I can hardly survive any more, thought Judy. Oh nature, nature who left out my instinct for self-survival and gave me this grudging betrayal of selfishness instead. When she finally quietened them down, they sulked but with the confidence of children who know for what they are crying. Tomorrow is Sunday, she said and in the morning we'll all travel out to

Spiddal and you'll play your whistle Tom for Furaisti and Pete with the bent nose will be there. Tom was the easiest to bring back, to forgive in a slow mechanical way the world that threatened to overwhelm him. It will be more wonderful than any Fleadh. Yes. And you have no more school for a fortnight, maybe more. Will the flute player be there from England, Tom proferred slowly, the one who wears the bicycle clips. Yes. Aye. All your father's friends.

— Sleep now ye pair.

And Friday was sitting quietly in the shed beside the duchess who occasionally looked up at him and night was there too except there was no sound only the sharp cries of the nightbirds from down the fields.

— That's a lovely daughter you've got there, the landlady said when Judy opened the door to see who was tiptoeing annoyingly across the landing. Then to silk she washed herself, her first warm bath for months under the watchful eyes of the awful blue staring fish and afterwards she draped herself luxuriously before a small electric fire. The glow from her flesh pleased her as did the silence and the small breaths of the sleeping. When she had left Belfast she had sworn she would never live in a city again, not for a day, but Galway she never really accepted as a city, it was more like a big drifting market town. She and her husband were changing, she knew. In Belfast they were satisfied politically, in that their bodies, like anyone else, could stop a bullet, but living so close to the south was a totally new beginning, a loveplay, something they had forgotten as she had forgotten that in the south what appeared trivial, negative to her was a natural way of life for a people unaffected by war. But her spirit had once enlarged, as her sister's now had. Still she worried about their farmhouse in Fermanagh constantly, even when she went to the village with the kids she always searched the now familiar trees for smoke, as if in a way she needed a ritual, a gradual dismemberment.

Eileen turned in her sleep.

The wind in the wires outside reminded Judy of home, like the sound of distant geese, she rubbed her body in front of the fire as the evening drew on.

— Politics is the last thing in the world I want to hear

about, said McFarland in a pub where he was the centre of attraction as he laid his fiddle down. The very last thing.

— Give us a slow air, someone interrupted in Salthill as they went from Toss the Feathers to The Flowers of Spring. And the bank manager danced to the tune.

— Everybody in the north wants to get on TV or into politics, a fisherman just in off the trawlers joked in The Largeys where an Irish soldier was playing the pipes in the backroom.

— Galway never changes.

— *Ni bhíonn ac súil amháin ag na nGael anois*, said Furaisti softly as they sat ruminating under Conaire in the square and watched a peculiar crowd spreading out from the railway station after arriving on the last train from Dublin. McFarland was restless, spending money recklessly. Saul had said, 'If I died tonight wouldn't you heel up the clothes and the money, and say didn't he hold onto it tight.' And he had left nothing but the view from the hill. McFarland remembered his own youth as warmth under a slated roof from the heavy rain, a vague wish on the side of a lake, and now returning years later to the house built like a church with its arched porch and stained-glass windows taken by bicycle from Donegal, he was learning the names for sounds he was born into, a tern fleeing from the rushes, milk churns rattling over the evening echo of the lake, a pheasant remembering the balls in her tail running over the mossy earth and perching on a fence to allow her scent bubble over the dogs, a perch bent in the scale-wet hands of his son. Oh history is a great time saver, a repellent against honest thought. There was no release, not like the falling release of a larch breaking at last under the swing of a steady axe, the shivers showering the earth.

— You know, Furaisti, you could hardly make ceiling laths from the trees in these parts, he said.

— Have you put down any vegetables the year, asked Furaisti.

— No. Next year for certain, he answered.

The dog slept by the cat in the shed and once he awoke and chased some shots off into the dark and the duchess stirred and smiled when he returned and sank beside her in the straw.

The radiators had filled the room with heavy cumbersome heat when Eileen heard the bomb open the sky in her sleep. A god filling in his time that she darted from on the verge of frightened dreams. She sank beneath the bed-clothes when she awoke, silent awhile till, as her panic grew more terrible, she called to her mother in the expressionless dark. Judy came in naked from the other room and wiped the blood from her bewildered daughter's face. In this strange house, even for a day, we have to start out all over again, relearning those familiar parts of ourselves that resist even the gentlest analysis and praying for a timely scepticism. As if as a child one had walked into a wet crumbling house and felt the tang of decay, emptiness, drab sky. The scar on her own white body ran like the shadow of a man's arm from beneath her childfallen breasts to the small warmth of her loins. I'd look fine, she thought as she comforted the child, on the inside pages of *Playboy* with my arms thrown open in tensed surprise like the cormorants we saw shading the waves from the island today. She threw open a window and pulled a deep orange robe over herself to get a drink downstairs for Eileen. The house was quiet. The boy in jeans and shirt was washing dishes in the kitchen and as he looked at her casually under his dark eyelids, she thought I'll take his mop of hair and squeeze his face between my legs so that he might scarcely breathe.

— I want to go home, said Eileen.

— Sleep now, the mother said and brushed Eileen's hair with her fingertips.

Judy walked through the sparse crowds, perhaps less euphoric now as they came into winter, their stale stomachs excruciated after the happy outrage of the long summer drinking, the headlights of a car brushing against the virginia creeper that nestled against the old university walls. She had hoped they might have driven out tonight to watch the wind spend itself on the dawn-grey stones of Connemara. Oh the myths the northerners love, the places where the troops will lie down! The chagrin burning on men's faces who expect answers that will confirm their own existence. In a small hostelry, up the dishevelled stairs among loud bemured

98

students who flaunted an adopted Gaelic and what little knowledge of alcoholism they had, she drank pints of Guinness in the early flamboyant style of a girl celebrating new values and wisdom, eager for a person to steal a promise from the ennui of the drinkers. She interrupted conversations readily, her accent tending to be either American or from a corner of Kerry, unaware or scared of the laughter.

— Do you know that Will Byrne is a real old fountain-head, she said, mimicking McFarland's accent.

— Belfast is the spiritual centre of Europe, she told a doctor.

— Fuck ye away from that house, ye bastards, old Byrne was shouting out of his lighted window and the dogs were barking, the duchess breaking away with raised hair through the long wet grass from the circling flames.

Meanwhile Furaisti and McFarland were rolling a stolen barrel of beer into a nurse's flat. The older man was out of breath and they had broken some strings on the fiddle. Four Connemara men in hats and coats stood drinking in the corridor with them, talking indifferently and happily among the endless traffic of people. They had a thirst like a chimney with a good draw. It took a while for McFarland to see confirmed in him and among the others a sense of other realities than being Irish, drink should let the mind wander to the present even foregoing the recent if not altogether past. And leaving in the dead of night, his arm round a friend, Saul spoke again. 'Be like a fox boy, piss on your trail and scatter the drops to puzzle the scent.' So McFarland to the air of the flogging reel took various routes home. And in the hotel the sound of his footsteps still came up the stairs to him, going from door to door searching for his room. Her clothes were scattered in a line to the bed. 'I have never known a woman like her,' he said as he lifted the sheets to Judy's chin and tucked her in next Eileen. He sat on the bed looking at them. In a word, Bach. Lord it is enough when it please Thee bring my life to a close, he placed the fiddle and bow on the chair. He read a few pages of Scott's travels, but his mind wandered to the time they alighted on Portaferry strand among the sunning ladies from the seagulls' clamour all night and all day, with a single seal dipping and spreading a long straight line on the ocean and how he thought that day his eyes might never focus again.

My trouble. In a word. Never lie on the left side, boy, you'll squeeze the heart out of yourself. Tom awoke and saw the match flare up in the dark and light up his father's face who had climbed awkwardly into bed beside him.

McFarland smoked in the darkness.

— Judy, Judy he whispered across.

— Are you awake, Judy?

— I heard tonight a story when Furaisti played the Banished Misfortune. It happened back in the days when death wasn't an institution. Jimmy Cummins turned to me and said Do you hear that. Well there was a fine piper from Gurteen, a fine piper in his day who drank nothing but French wine and oddly enough just played once in a fine house. He'd mind that night if he were alive today. For there the gentry's daughter came away with him, a lightsome girl and the parents naturally enough with acres of turnips and cabbages for setting disowned her. There was no hue or cry and the Gurteen man took her on his short travels for money and baby clothes. For the girl was expecting a piper's baby and not long after she and the baby died in this town. The coffin was put up on a cart drawn by a dray horse and no one following from the cobbles of the Spanish Arch. And the piper began to play a lament, not too slow or not quick on account of his losses, and the men in the fever hospital sweating from their labours counted four thousand mourners as they crossed Loch Ataile for Forthill graveyard. That's the Banished Misfortune for you, said Jimmy Cummins.

— Do you hear me Judy?

She heard him in a drunken vulgar way, accessible still for all his various frailties but she was silent for in her heart of hearts she feared he was softening, losing his sense of justice, merely protesting that erratic comedy of life. Fear was so addictive, consuming all of a body's time and she wanted so much to share this vigil with him in Fermanagh but what could you give the young if they were barricaded from the present by our lyrical, stifling past. She said nothing, knowing she shared this empty ecstasy with a thousand others who had let their laziness go on too long.

— I left home too young, that's what bothers me, he spoke again. There must be a thousand stories and songs about my own place that I hardly know. But when we return, woman, we'll try.

In a foot of land there's a square mile of learning, Saul had said, and he had learned to build from a sense of duty to the beauty of the hilly Erne.

For in April of 1910, Saul had a bad back but nevertheless he had finished building a church in Donegal town and now with Bimbo Flynn the whistler he set about kissing the air and erecting his own house. And it was a house where the best sessions of music would be held, where you could drive a tractor through the back windows. They gathered the red limestone rocks from the hills and fine washed stones from the Erne, the broached flagstones from Sliabh Buadh. Are you after work, he asked the grimy gypsies. God, you might swear mister, they said, and the gypsies carried cartloads of rocks up the hillside and sat under the chestnut tree smoking and drinking while it rained. His wife Olive came from the old house each day with tea and sandwiches for the men taking their time at their work on the edge of the woods that fell away to the lake. He'll fire everything to get back to America, the neighbours said knowing the long travelling of the McFarlands but as summer came he straightened up like a post in the good weather and the roof edged across the sky.

— Let it pass by.
— Judy.
— Piss on them, boy, piss on them.
— Where are we for today then?
— Men of Ireland.
— Do him no good to be a fife player now.
— I'd kill a man for that.
— Look, we'll hang the door tomorrow.
— Have done with it.

When the burning was a long time off they put in two rows of slates as a damp course and timbered each room from the yellow larch that crashed in a fine storm, Bimbo never tiring of the saw that sang in his hands, his feet muffled in the knee-high sawdust and the briars in the hair of the gypsy children. A bird nested in the bodhran young Will Byrne,

101

a great lad, had left in his father's barn. Boys oh boys. And in July a stray Dalmatian came whistling up through the grass to them of a Friday, his spots like squashed blackberries, jumping round himself. They adopted him for the new house. The iron shone on the range and the whistler fenced off an orchard and set forty apple trees and Olive took great care putting down their first rose bush. And folks wondered about the ornamented porch that was built out front with the stained-glass windows, and there was talk of a church but when the last stones dried and you could hear the knock-knock of a thrush breaking a snail in his new garden Saul was a proud man. Always before daylight a man thinks of his destiny, as Saul did that last morning talking with the travellers in the half light of the chestnut hill and he was glad to see that the cream-coloured mare of the gypsies was loth to leave the fine grass now that her time had come.

Compassion

ITA DALY

As I look back over the years — some thirty years from young adulthood until now — I know one thing with certainty. I know that I have grown in compassion. It is pleasant to feel that there *is* some plus quantity in the midst of all the wreckage; and it is a feeling that many of my age-group may share. For although it is obviously true that some young people are tolerant and have pity to spare, I do not think, on the whole, that compassion comes naturally to the young. They are too preoccupied with their own griefs and problems to pause long enough to consider the condition of others. Today, I always endeavour to look behind the façade, to seek out the wounded soul lurking there. And I usually find it. Is it the competitiveness of youth that makes it so eager to condemn?

Twenty-four years ago I was teaching in a large Dublin school. At least it was considered large in those days, and very modern and progressive. Perhaps it was in order to give some substance to this reputation for modernity that Mother de Lourdes, the mistress of schools, employed mainly a young lay staff. Certainly it was unusual, at that time, to find five women, all under thirty, employed in a Convent Secondary School.

I was somewhat older than the others — I was twenty-nine then — and I know that two of them were straight from College, which would put them at no more than twenty-two. But despite the age differences, we were all very close. We became tremendous friends, spending a great deal of time in each other's company. Two of us were from Dublin, one from Cork, one from Limerick, and one, Peggy, a native Irish-speaker from the Donegal Gaeltacht.

Even at that time the teaching profession had, for many years, been an acceptable escape route for the deserving working class. The bright, hard-working small-farmer's or labourer's son, while he could never hope to become a doctor or an architect, could always gain a foothold into the middle classes by becoming a teacher. But this was, I think, less true for women teachers, and particularly University-trained women teachers, and we five in the Convent of Jesus Our Saviour appeared as middle-class as you could find. Our bourgeois aura encompassed us, and although today we might be considered a smug lot, this smugness, as with many middle-class people, arose from ignorance — lack of imagination rather than any real arrogance. My father was a lawyer; his father had been a comfortable farmer from the Golden Vale. As a family we accepted financial ease and an educated background as we accepted the colour of our eyes or the green of the grass. The other four, I had always assumed, came from similar backgrounds. I knew that Joan did, for I had spent one summer in her Sunday's Well home, a tall gracious house, like mine full of heavy mahogany furniture, but with a magnificent view up the river Lee.

And I think there was a certain basis for my assumption, for despite the romantic notion that we Irish have of ourselves of making one leap from the peasant's cabin to the good job in the Civil Service, scores of Irish families have, like my own, been sending sons to Clongowes College for three generations. The interesting thing about this class is that it is totally nationalistic in outlook. Despite the best efforts of the Jesuits there are no Englishmen *manqué* here, and I know that my family has always been conscious of its Irish identity, and proud of it. It may have been this outlook, present in all of us, which caused a certain insensitivity in our reaction to, and therefore treatment of, Peggy.

By the time she arrived in the school, Joan, Rita, Shiela and I had already coalesced into a sort of group, a coterie. Our friendship had taken on a formality, and with this an obligation, so that we were like members of a very exclusive club. But we were cultural snobs, and I think the first thing that struck any of us about Peggy was that she would lend a certain distinction to our group. We considered that we had become friends because we were civilized people in an uncivilized world. Accordingly, we set ourselves a fairly rigid code of behaviour. Our interests being intellectual, we never permitted ourselves to read women's magazines or listen to popular music on the radio. We patronized the theatre extensively, and the cinema selectively. We never boasted of money or holidays or boy-friends. In fact, it was an unwritten rule that boy-friends were mentioned only in the most oblique fashion, and we observed this rule faithfully, both out of consideration for any member of the group who might not have a boy-friend, and out of disdain for anything that might smell of one-upmanship. Our victories were always moral. At the time Peggy joined us I was enjoying a particular moral distinction, for I had just captured — temporarily, as it turned out — the most eligible bachelor in town. He was a young University don whose work in the field of literary criticism was making people in England and America sit up and take notice. He was never mentioned by me to one of the group except as 'a friend of mine,' and I would feel a glow of satisfaction as Joan would look at me, first appraisingly, and then with approval. It appeared to us that our subtleties knew no bounds.

Anyone reading this may see us as young prigs, but I think such a view would be unkind and unjust. There was nothing particularly wrong with our life style, and there was much that was admirable in our idealism — it was simply that we took ourselves and each other so seriously. Most young people do, and we were determined to leave our mark on life. We were also totally loyal to each other. In school we exchanged ideas, helped one another with work, covered up if one of us was late. Outside school we always spent Wednesday evenings and Sunday afternoons together, all five of us. We adhered strictly to this routine and none of us would dream of making a date for either of these days. Otherwise we kept our lives largely apart. I think now that the reason for this was that such austerity had to be tempered by a more relaxing style of living during the rest of the week.

Wednesday evenings were devoted to our cultural sorties, and after some time we achieved through them a certain acclaim. As a group we shared above average good looks, and we all believed in *la bella figura,* but on Wednesday evenings it had to be a corporate one. Thus, before we set out to a concert, or a theatre or a cinema we would plan carefully together what each one would wear. The group must look distinguished, the figures must blend; as in dressing a play, the total effect was what was important. Then we would appear together, the five of us, in the foyer of a cinema or theatre, smiling, slightly distant, absorbed in ourselves. Our conversations on such occasions had a formality too, and it was understood that they would be serious, carried on in measured tones, no idle chatter.

How we enjoyed discussing afterwards the sensation we had caused. Sometimes someone well-known would be discovered eyeing us with interest, and the speculation would become wild: we would undoubtedly appear in a poem, be the mysterious heroines of some play. The effect we had on men delighted us. We would note the admiring glances, and then the puzzlement. We felt as we thought film-stars must feel, and we all agreed that it was totally understandable that one man could never hope to satisfy such as them.

Sunday afternoons were spent either in my house or Rita's, we being the only two with homes in Dublin. I had a bedroom on the top floor of our house, looking out over the garden to the mountains beyond. I turned it into a bed-sittingroom, filling it with large silk cushions, swathing my electric light bulbs in downy pink, fixing adhesive round the door and windows to exclude draughts. Before the others arrived I'd light a log fire, and by four o'clock the room was scented, softly shadowed and warm. With a record playing mutedly on the gramophone, it was an oasis of comfort and security in the gloom of a winter afternoon. At five, Elsie would bring the tea.

It was all rather affected, but quite harmless. I'm sure I saw myself as a literary hostess and my bedsit as my salon. We were all afflicted with extreme self-consciousness so that even drinking a cup of tea became a ritual. But how we enjoyed ourselves at our tea-parties and our outings. Life has never held the same piquancy for me since, and anytime nowadays that I smell China tea, I am instantly transported back to those Sunday afternoons.

When Peggy had been a month or so in the school, we

asked her to join us one weekend. She arrived at my house earlier than the others, and sat like a mouse all through the afternoon. She never lost this shyness, and even when she had known us for eight or nine months she still never proferred an opinion or suggested a particular play or film that we should see. We found this altogether charming, and she became the pet of the group, protected by the rest of us, indulged in her difference.

Later however, she began to assert herself in the most distressing manner. The second year, when she came back after the summer holidays, we noticed a change at once. She looked different for a start, brighter, harder, almost common. She immediately launched into an account of her marvellous holiday in Venice. We were prepared to forgive her — we suspected that it was the first time she had been abroad, and we approved of her choice. But then, for our first Wednesday outing, she turned up in a most outrageous dress, scarlet and shining and deeply décolleté. It was quite appalling, and none of us could understand it, for as usual we had planned our corporate ensemble, and had all decided on muted autumnal tones, particularly suitable for the first week in September. She looked at us brazenly as she walked into the theatre, sweeping back her head like a filly. It was a lapse, but we would accept it. It was perhaps natural that Peggy might feel swamped by the rest of us and was now simply making an effort to assert herself. But we wished she had done it with more taste. The incident would have been forgotten if her continuing behaviour hadn't forced us to realize that something would have to be done.

Now, not satisfied with monopolizing every conversation, she began to name-drop blatantly. She would tell us that she had had cocktails last week with Professor so-and-so, or that she had spent the previous evening discussing contemporary art with some well-known sculptor. We decided that Joan was the one to take her in hand. She was particularly kind and fine-grained, and could be trusted to point things out to Peggy without hurting her feelings. We never thought simply of dropping her; we were fond of her and she was one of us. Joan assured us that we need have no worries — she would do her best and we must continue to treat Peggy as if nothing were amiss.

She was as good as her word. Within three weeks we could see a change in Peggy's behaviour. She ceased to boast, and she began to dress more quietly again, more in harmony with the group. We were pleased. But our pleasure was to be short lived, for soon Peggy was showing other, more disturbing, signs. She became very withdrawn, worse than when she had come to Dublin first. She never spoke at all unless we asked her something, and her former interest in our activities now turned to listlessness. But she still insisted on coming everywhere with us and doing everything that we did. Another meeting was obviously called for, and so one evening the rest of us sat down around my parents' dining table, believing that the seriousness of the occasion demanded something less frivolous than my bedroom.

At the end of three hours we decided that it was we who must have been at fault. Joan was convinced that she was particularly to blame. She felt that Peggy must have been offended by some comment she had made. She had tried to be careful, to think of every possible interpretation of everything she said, but now she felt that, obviously, she had not succeeded. The rest of us, however, could not agree with this. We were all responsible and we should have realized long ago how shy and timid Peggy was and let her continue in her absurd fashion if she had to. As the eldest of the group I felt a special responsibility, and I decided I'd take her under my wing from then on. I would bring her out more on her own, even encourage her to talk about her famous boy-friends. I was determined to make amends.

And I did. I took to walking home from school with her, and I'd ask her about her boy-friends, and tell her how pretty she was and how much I envied her her lovely hair. I took her out to see my aunt in Monkstown, where I hoped my cousin Larry, who was about her own age, might become interested in her. That day was a disaster however, for Peggy was at her worst, spilling her sherry and staring round her like a terrified sheep. I wanted to shake her but I had to feel sorry for her too — she was obviously going through agonies. I took her out to tea and coffee, and indeed I was soon devoting the major portion of my leisure time to her.

But I didn't mind too much. I was still experiencing pangs of guilt, and felt that it was no more than just that I should be inconvenienced as punishment for my transgression. The others all helped of course, and gradually our patience began to pay off. Peggy became less withdrawn; she began to offer opinions readily and altogether seemed to grow more relaxed in our company. And, although she lapsed occasionally, she seemed to be boasting less. One evening Joan suggested that it would be a good idea if we asked her to give us Irish lessons. It would be a boost to her ego, and she'd feel at last that *she* had something to teach *us*. Besides, it might be quite fun. Shiela agreed and said that as she'd forgotten her Irish, she'd welcome the opportunity of learning some again. Peggy seemed pleased enough, and so, from then on, on every second Sunday we had two hours of Irish conversation. Rita and Shiela, who had some acting ability, would often improvise a little play, Rita with a scarf round her head as a shawl acting out the part of the long-suffering wife, and Shiela, with a cap specially bought for the purpose, promising her that he would give up the drink. Or some such nonsense.

These antics had been going on for about five months – none of us learning much Irish but having tremendous fun – when one evening after school Mother de Lourdes summoned Joan and myself to her office. She handed us a brown envelope, dog-eared and with her name scrawled on it. 'Open it,' she said, 'and read it.' Inside, written in clumsy block capitals on a piece of cheap lined note-paper, were the words, 'Do you know what kind of women you are employing? Ask them what corruption they get up to at their get-togethers.' Naturally, it was unsigned.

We were so shocked that neither of us could say anything for some moments, and then we both broke out together, crying inarticulately of our disgust, our revulsion at such obscenity. Mother de Lourdes took us both by the hand and tried to calm us. 'I know, my dears, I know how you must feel. It is quite appalling, but you had to know. I couldn't rest tonight with that . . . thing lying on my desk. Now that I've told you, I am going to burn it and forget about it and say a prayer for whoever perpetrated such a deed. They need prayer. Let us all try to forget about it.'

But we were not allowed to do so. Next morning Mother de Lourdes received another note and the morning after that, another. The letters were always shoved under the convent door, presumably at night — the wall at the end of the drive was low and easy to get across even when the gates were locked at ten. Over and over again we asked ourselves who could have sent them. Who could hate us enough to want to? The insinuations were vague in all three letters, but in a sense this made them worse, for the hints of decadence and evil were more upsetting than a specific accusation. We were all girls who had been surrounded with love and admiration all our lives and what stunned us most was the venom of the writer.

Then on the sixth day of that terrible week, Joan came to me before class, white-faced and trembling. She drew me aside and handed me the now familiar bit of paper. I took it and spread it out.

'You think you have a nice cushy set-up you and your friend Anne Tierney but the joke's on you. Her father fucks her every night. Ask her how she likes it.'

Of course, we couldn't show this to Mother de Lourdes — it was too horrifying for anyone else to see — but equally we could not let it go any further. God knows what might happen if this continued. We decided on a plan which we would carry out ourselves. The letters to the convent were delivered by hand, presumably sometime after the nuns had gone to bed. All Joan and I had to do was lie in wait behind the rhododendron bushes near the front door. We would stay there till dawn if necessary.

The first night we took up our positions, armed with flasks of coffee and woollen rugs. We arrived at nine-thirty and were well dug in by the time Dan the handyman went down to lock the gates. At half-past ten we saw the lights go out one by one in the nuns' cells. Our vigil was long and cold and fruitless. By the time dawn was breaking, we were frozen and sleepy, and not a thing had passed up the driveway, not even a stray cat. Saturday night followed the same pattern and on Sunday we were prepared for another sleepless vigil and were both dreading the thought of a full day's school next morning. By twelve o'clock Joan was nodding off beside me but I was too cold and too cramped to be able even to rest in comfort. As I drew the rug closer around me, suddenly I heard, from the direction of the gate, the scuffing of gravel. It was a still night and the footsteps that now started up the driveway were magnified in the silence. I nudged Joan awake, and we sat there, clutching one another, shaking with terror. The footsteps approached inexorably, and then, Peggy stepped out in front of us into a shaft of moonlight. I could see her profile and the fair sheen of her hair. She was wearing the plaid coat that she always wore to school. We both started forward. 'Peggy,' we gasped involuntarily. She turned quickly in the direction of our voices, and recognizing us even in the shadows, wheeled abruptly round and broke into a run. As she ran, something fell from her hand. We knew what it would be before we went to retrieve it. There was no need to open the brown envelope.

We never mentioned Peggy again. Next day we told everything to Mother de Lourdes, and within hours there was a vacancy for an Irish teacher in the Convent of Jesus Our Saviour. We had to tell Rita and Shiela also, but once we had done so the matter was closed. Shortly afterwards, the group began to break up. We did have one tea-party in my bedsitting room but it was not a success. We were all painfully embarrassed and glad when it was time to go. That July I applied for a post in Wicklow.

Two years later I had bought a new car and was visiting an aunt of mine in Sligo. When I was there I suddenly realized how near I was to Donegal, and on impulse I decided to drive up. I had no definite plan, but after a day's driving I found myself in Peggy's townland. I had no fear of meeting Peggy, for I had heard indirectly that she was still in the local mental hospital where she had been sent after her breakdown on leaving Dublin. I knew she had a sister called Annie whom she had often talked about, and I stopped at the post-office and asked the post-mistress for directions to Annie McMenamin's house.

The road that I took was full of pot-holes and twisted through bleak and barren bog. After about two miles it began to peter out, and I thought I had been misdirected, when I saw on my right, sheltered by a few deformed trees, a low whitewashed cottage. It was little bigger than our tool-shed at home, and not as well built. The front walls had been discoloured by cow-dung and the tiny windows were curtainless. In front of the door, a few hens pecked dispiritedly in the mud. Suddenly the door opened and a man appeared. He was wearing a collarless shirt and his trousers were held up with twine. He was carrying an enamel basin and he emptied its contents over a stunted hedge. Then he paused, cleared his nose between finger and thumb, and this too went over the hedge. The door was slammed shut again and the hens continued to peck.

I looked at Peggy's home, and I remembered with a painful sharpness all those Sunday afternoons of two years ago. I remembered Peggy McMenamin and the disintegration of our dream. And do you know what I felt as I looked at the desolate scene? I felt resentment. Not pity, not understanding — much less compassion. Nothing but resentment.

The Quizmasters of St Patcheen's

SEAN MacMATHUNA
(translated from the Irish by the author)

I lived in an old house by the river. Except for the swish of
the water and the rafters which creaked in the cold, it was
a silent house. At night things moved in the weeds. In winter
I stood to my ankles in the cooling snow and gazed in
wonder at the beauty of my house. In summer farmers
gathered with implements to cut the things that had chanced
to grow, releasing their sweet quick on the dry air. They
planked their misshapen faces on the fence. 'Let us kill your
weeds for you,' they implored, waving billhooks and sickles
in the air. I smiled with contempt at them.

I sat in my house and listened to the thistles knock at my
window in a breeze, reminding me that I do not meddle, that
I do no violence to this earth. This creed left my house in
disarray but it is better to live in squalor with a philosophy
than to be tidy and in pain.

I worked in a funny place: The Quiz school of St
Patcheen. The Quizmasters were all funny too. If they saw
me laugh they shook their fists in anger and scolded me.

'Shirker, layabout, get some work done.' One doesn't
laugh in a funny school. There were also 325 brats in my
school.

Brutus Iscariot was the headmaster; some said he was an
escaped priest. He was very involved in the community.
Every morning he put a 'Do Not Disturb' sign on his door
and shinned down the drainpipe at the back of the school.
I waited for him there one morning to discuss with him the
matter of my money, which was in arrears. He came down
with a thump, surprised.

'Oh, it's you, you feckless lazybones. When are you going
to stop swinging the lead, pull up your socks, get off your ass
and get down to the nitty gritty?'

113

'I've sent for some new quizzes,' I said. Then I paused for words. Should I call my money a stipend, gratuity, or honorarium? It was always in Latin, all part of the insult.

'What about my pay?' I blurted out. He gave me the humourless smile of the escaped priest.

'Why do Quizmasters think so much about their pay, and so little about their reward?' and he squinted slyly up to heaven. Then he was gone in a flash down the boreen to say Mass or open a dog show.

The Quizmasters never stayed out sick. Every morning they presented themselves for duty with crushing repetition. Nor did they ever interfere with the running of the school, except once in their lives; that's the day the Great Inspector himself came to visit. They say the angel of death is so busy in schools that he wears a mortar board; but he is efficient and kind to teachers. One great farewell thump in the chest, chalky hands grasp the air, before your brave pedagogue keels over to achieve the Great Horizontal. There he lies fallen until discovered by charwomen. But if the brats in their desks liked the Quizmaster, one usually went to Brutus and shouted, 'Another cardiac arrest in room 5A.' The brats were well used to the discipline of Quizmasters' funerals and their behaviour was good; for they would rather follow a Quizmaster to his grave than follow him down the grey road of the third declension.

It is easy to fill a Quizmaster's position. Take Cerberus, for instance. He was originally trained for the jail next door to St Patcheen's, but he came in the wrong gate. Brutus immediately banished him to the classroom. They say old Cerberus never knew the difference. At night he wandered through the corridors communicating with doors and locks. Brutus got most of his teachers like that, anybody who came to the door, plumbers, gravediggers, and Jehovah's Witnesses. The butcher's boy was terrified of Brutus. His latest plan was to hang the sausages on the door-knocker and run. It was also because of Brutus' little habit that no inspectors would visit the school.

All the Quizmasters had long shadows but Rigormortis beat them all. He was very thin and carried a shadow twenty-three feet long. I know because I measured it one day when

114

he wasn't looking. When he came in in the morning his shadow was in front of him spying out the corridor, but in the evening he had to drag it all the way out into the twilight. The other Quizmasters said that Rigormortis' shadow wasn't his own but belonged to something that had died. It was bad luck to step on it. He never approached the staff-shed in the yard but took his lunch by himself in the stone corridor. There he sat erect among the Ogham stones, his bony fingers filching bread from a paper bag, masticating each bite thirty times. He was proud of his thirty mastications and resulting good health. Rigormortis had no nickname; for Rigormortis could be likened to nothing but things could be likened to Rigormortis, like Celtic crosses and Ogham stones.

Size is very important; people don't realize that. I'm always measuring things. Interruptus, the first day he came to the Quiz school on his tricycle, was all of four and a half feet. He was unusually energetic; tall Quizmasters had to be wary of him or they were chinned in the crotch. One day when we were in the queue for our free pencils and rubbers, I noticed that Interruptus, who was in front of me, came up only to the bottom button of my waistcoat. When I explained to him that he was diminishing and would shortly have to be replaced, he disagreed with me. After that Interruptus cut me dead but took to wearing large hats. Nobody likes the truth.

Neither did Sufferinjaysus. Nobody ever spoke to Sufferinjaysus when they met him in the corridors, they just grunted in sympathy. He quizzed in a room with the curtains continually drawn. Two fires heated two generations of sweaty, adolescent BO and Vick. Sufferinjaysus was concerned about his health. He stood in the room with his back to the fire and tossed Euclidian cuts to the brats. We borrowed fag-ends from each other; but when I heard his Local Defence Force boots drag in the corridor I had to be wary; to this day I think he owes me three. He was at his best in a pub when he enthused about body building courses, and laughter, and sunshine in his childhood. But he was not graceful. I always say that those who are neither graceful nor elegant should be belted with porter bottles on the back of the head.

Vercingetorix was the greatest enigma of all. He was the

Latin Quizmaster and was so calm and composed at all times that I was suspicious. He never did anything wrong like being sick, laughing or having a cardiac arrest. But his brothers told me his secret. Every Friday Vercingetorix covered the dining room table with copybooks to be corrected. The brothers, all six of them, bachelors, played poker by the fire. Suddenly something would happen to Vercingetorix's mind. For a split second in his week sanity took over. He would arise from the table trembling, looking strangely at the copybooks. 'I'm not a Quizmaster; I couldn't be one,' he'd say in revulsion.

'Yes you are,' the brothers would reply in unison.

'Well, I deserve a good walloping so.'

Immediately the brothers would rush upon him, fetching him clouts and wallops until they brought him to the ground; while on the ground the oldest brother, who was a dwarf and had to wait his turn, would kick him in the crotch. Vercinge-torix would then pass out with a delighted groan. After a while he'd pick himself up, the calmest man in Academia.

Ah, but Miss Parnassus, dear, darling Miss Parnassus. She is a born Quizmistress, quite literally. When she was seven days old her parents put chalk into her hand, and her dear little fist closed on it so tightly they couldn't feed her for days. I'm in love with Miss Parnassus. I wasalways asking her for chalk so that I could touch her, my little finger tarrying in her chalky palm. What a treat I say! She has a little hair on the tip of her nose that I would dearly like to play with. I was always pressing my rulers on her. I never gave rulers to anyone else. As a result I had lots and lots of them in my press, rulers of every kind, mind you. But she didn't seem to need them. I need them myself for measuring.

One day I told Miss Parnassus that I had a little house by the river in the country. She didn't seem interested. But because she is a born Quizmistress I knew she would relent when I told her about my invention for correcting essays. We went out on a Spring day and walked in pedagogical communion by the river banks, she remarking on how gaily the little verbs twittered in their conjugations, while I pointed out the tidy nests the nouns built in their declensions.

My little house stood out, proud of its greenery. Her face

began to harden as she picked her way through my weeds. She almost balked at the briars at the front door. I took my Miss Parnassus into my house, a real live woman in my house. I almost felt weak. I hastened to her needs, dusting chairs for her, putting on the kettle, rinsing a cup for her and cushing the flies out the window. She stood in the middle of the floor, her eyes narrowing at the disarray of my parlour. I sat at her feet and gaped up at her, my eyes imploring some kindness.

'Why don't you kill those filthy weeds?' she asked. I lectured her on labels, pointing out that weeds were careless flowers, that the word weed was divisive and suggestive of a rank (no pun) that did not exist, that I preferred the word 'plant' for all green things.

'Well, why don't you clean up this?' she said, sweeping her hand in contempt at my little disarray. I looked about me and said that the things in my environment could depend on me not to destroy them. While the iron was hot I showed her my invention. From a purple box I took out four rubber stamps. On each was written respectively, 'Very good', 'Very bad', 'Not so good', 'Not so bad'.

I grabbed a bundle of copies that had been in the corner for years and attacked them with the rubber stamps, each correction raising a cloud of dust.

'This is revolutionary,' I said with excitement and Miss Parnassus began to cough. In no time at all I despatched forty of the wretched things back into the corner. But poor Miss Parnassus, she was still coughing and her eyes were red. She said she had 'flu and had to go. I escorted her tenderly to the door.

The next day I went to Miss Parnassus' room and with a big smile asked her for chalk. She said she had none. I retreated in consternation to my own roomful of brats. There I did a lot of thinking. I decided that if I were to be successful I would have to rearrange my furnishings, do some dusting perhaps.

That evening I wandered through the rooms of my house, noting the soiled shirts, the coffee stains, the cigarette ash, old shoes and dirty socks, beds that had never been made, broken delph and mildew. It was no use, I could not raise my hand against them.

So it went for days, reflecting, contemplating, vacillating, round and round my head went in agonizing circularity.

It happened on Friday. As soon as I opened the door I smelt it: floor polish. I opened my eyes wide at the shining hall. I inched my way in, in dread. All the floors shone like plates, walls scrubbed down, furniture polished and arranged in a pleasing fashion, neat rows of shining delph on the dresser, and the bathroom smelt of flowers. But I nearly lost my mind when I saw the bed. White starched sheets, pillows puffed out with pride, eiderdown arranged artistically. I took one jump and landed in the middle of it, yelping with joy, burying my face in the white coolness of the sheets. It was like an iced cake and I could have eaten it. I jumped and frolicked and tossed my pyjamas in the air. It brought me back to my childhood and the smell of the bread in the oven. Suddenly I got up and looked about me. Then I pranced around the house examining doors and windows. Everything was intact.

I have a host of good friends who would only be too willing to do all this in lieu of the many kindnesses which it is my nature to perform, but after a second glance I realized that this had been done by a woman. Bang went the friends theory. It was of course Miss Parnassus. Yes, I decided, this was performed out of love.

Next day I didn't ask her for any chalk. It is always better to let these things happen naturally. I stayed in my room smiling knowingly and listening for her dainty walk in the corridor. The brats were sniggering, they were quick to catch on to something. I don't mind, in love one can be tolerant. I even promised them new quizzes.

A few days later she had been there again. There were two laundry bags in the bathroom with labels attached to them, 'Coloureds', 'Whites'. In the kitchen delph was laid out for a meal. I was very pleased with her work, and I yelped with lonesome glee. I went on my now accustomed pilgrimage through the rooms, sniffing, and feeling, and peering at myself in mirrors. Then I noticed my whiskey. With great misgivings I extracted a ruler from my pocket and measured. I was right, there were about four half ones missing. I slept very poorly that night for I would not be pleased with a tippling woman for a wife.

On the following Monday I rushed home on my bicycle without even bothering to fasten the clips on my trousers. More whiskey was gone and some food. I didn't mind about the food. Then I saw a note on the mantelpiece, 'Use the ashtrays please'. She was so right in a way. I was proud of the house, I was pleased with her work, but the whiskey was another matter. I decided to go to her the following day and have it out with her.

But alas, next day old Semper Virens, the Irish Quizmaster, achieved the Great Horizontal in the middle of the past subjunctive. He had been sitting so long in his oaken rostrum that bark encased his knees. It had been decided that should he take root he should be cut down and made into rulers, a commodity in sore supply in my school. But no plans were ready. As they took old Semper Virens out through the hall in his coffin, Brutus Iscariot was livid with rage.

'Jesus Christ, what a day to get a hea— . . . a cardiac arrest. Six weeks to the Leaving Certificate; where will it all end?' Only Semper Virens knew. Brutus had to give us all a half day and both brats and Quizmasters ran for the gate in high glee.

I went early to the house and that's how I discovered it all. There was a man in my kitchen with an apron on; he was washing dishes by the sink and hummed idly to himself. He didn't even look up.

'Who on earth are you and what are you doing in my house?' I was outraged. He had an unusual calmness about him which I found cheeky. His eyes were cold and expressionless. He never answered, just continued to hum in an empty fashion.

'Where did you get the key to come into my house?' I said, not without anger.

'I didn't come in,' he said, 'I was here always.'

'Now, now,' I said, 'I'll have none of that, not in my house.' I was quite firm, a quality I have learned from my profession.

'Come,' he said peremptorily. I followed him out to the

119

hallway. 'Look,' he said and he pointed up at the attic trap door. It was open, and I gazed up at the square darkness.

'I never saw that before. You came down from there you say?'

'Yes, I have been there always, it's quite a nice place really.'

I found a step-ladder and climbed up. I stuck my head into that inky blackness and I immediately felt a strange calm.

'I can't see anything,' I said. 'It's very dark.'

'You don't have to see anything, that's why I'm up there. It's also quiet and peaceful and nobody bothers you.'

'I suppose you're right. Is it dry?'

'As dry as a haystack. There's great shelter up there. There's wood, felt, and slate between you and the weather.'

'How do you spend your time up there?'

'In thought.'

'You're right too. I'm worn out from thought myself, but it's great isn't it?'

I came down and we went back to the kitchen. I filled out whiskey for myself as I usually do in company. I think he looked rather perturbed about the whiskey, or maybe it was my feet.

'I'd appreciate it if you wouldn't put your feet on the table.'

I did as he said.

'I'd like you to know that you're doing a grand job here, and I'm very grateful.'

'You needn't be grateful but be careful.' And he danced off around the house, flicking pictures and ornaments with a rag.

'You have a nice house,' he called from the hallway. 'We both have,' I shouted back, but I heard the attic trap door bang. I was alone again. I walked around my little palace a few times, as proud as an archdeacon. It was as clean as the chalice. I made tea and called up to him but he didn't answer. I have noticed that people of great depth are like that. I drank my tea and watched my purple thistles dance in the breeze. Company is a great thing.

Next day I went into Miss Parnassus' room. She charmed me with a gorgeous blush. She spoke crossly to me but

I know that a good Quizmistress must be cross. I pressed some rulers on her but she refused. Then I spoke to her out of the side of my mouth about a certain house, telling her (and I winked at her) that it was a palace. The brats began to snigger and Miss Parnassus began to write on the blackboard. I shrugged at the brats and left the room.

I sat alone in the kitchen. After a while the man from the rafters alighted. He examined the house and I am proud to say it was perfect. While he helped himself to my whiskey I complained about Miss Parnassus.

'Have patience, man, you'll see her in this house yet.' He said it with such conviction that it fired my soul. I was getting fond of a man who could give such good advice.

For days I sat in my quizroom listening for her dainty walk in the corridor, knowing that each step brought her closer to me.

'What kind of work do you do?' he said one day to me. I explained about the Quiz school. But he wanted details. I explained about the importance of working at a higher level than the brats. He immediately stood on an old orange case.

'Like this?' I nodded. Then I explained about the quiz book in the Quizmaster's hand, and the quizzes.

'What sort of quizzes?'

'Oh,' I said, 'the usual thing: Who made the world? Depths of rivers, tombstones and anything generally about long ago.' He wanted to know what one did if they didn't answer.

'Correct them,' I said.

'How?'

'Roar,' I answered. The man from the rafters roared suddenly and gave me quite a fright.

'Is that all?' he asked. I mentioned the importance of learning to balance copybooks on the carrier of one's bicycle, of having at least three good jokes and of the folly of joining a pension scheme.

'Sure any old fool could do that,' he said. I hung my head with shame for I knew he spoke the truth, but my loyalty to the profession would not allow me to admit it.

On another occasion he said to me when he had alighted beside me, 'It grieves me to see a man of your potential and

121

undoubted talents slaving your life away day in, day out.'

The truth of the statement shocked me. I got up on unsteady feet and grasped his hand.

'You are a true friend.' His hand was cold.

'Isn't it time you took a day off?'

'It certainly is, but what excuse could I have?'

'Sick.'

'Can't go sick. It's not permitted.'

'How about a heart attack?'

'You may only have one cardiac arrest. He who has the second one is never forgiven.'

We were silent for some time. Suddenly he slapped his hands together.

'I have it: you stay here and I will go in your place.' It was a brilliant idea but it was dangerous.

'They'd be quick to catch on to something like that where I work. You'd be recognized.'

'How would I? They don't know me. Anyway, I'm good with disguises.' I was uncomfortable.

'I'd be missed, I think.'

'Maybe not, try it. Just think of it, you could take a week given over to thought. Furthermore, I invite you to go to the attic and really contemplate.'

That did it.

'Really, you wouldn't mind?'

'Certainly not, you are more than welcome.'

I was dying for a go at the attic; for too long I had been observing the man from the rafters and marvelling at what an attic could do for a man. With a mixture of foreboding and excitement I agreed, and we went to bed.

The sun was hardly up when the commotion in the kitchen awakened me; I trotted out in my bare feet. There he was on his knees with my rubber stamps, giving the copybooks hell.

'What's going on?'

'Correcting.'

'They've been there for years, some of those guys are dead.'

'It doesn't matter,' he said 'their parents might like a souvenir. Anyway, the place has to be cleared.'

I looked down at the battered, dogeared copies, stained

with beer and coffee on the outside, and inside a cemetery of useless information.

At eight-thirty he tottered to the door with copies and piled them on the carrier of my bike. As he was about to mount he called out to me, 'By the way, what's your name?'

'Anthropos, Mr Anthropos,' I shouted back as I watched him sway away to work. I had misgivings, but I felt exhilarated at the prospect of the attic.

I stuck my head through the square darkness of the trap and entered upon the black peace of freedom from the flesh. I lay on his rug and felt the fears and regrets and terrors of work rise off my bones as a fine dust and float away into the unknown abyss of the attic. I developed a theory about attics and the wonderful way that wood, felt and slate protected a body from the hostile vibrations that beset ordinary rooms.

The door-bang signalled me to emerge from that sweet well of release and to enter the world of foolish men again. I shoved my head down to welcome the man back but he was so busy with armfuls of copies that he didn't notice me. I alighted full of wonder at the world again and I followed him into the room.

'Well, how did the day go?' I said as I picked up a fistful of copies and flung them into the corner as is my wont. The man from the rafters grew very flustered at this and ran to the corner to retrieve them. He restacked them again. The copies were new and had freshly inked work on them.

'Got to keep the place tidy,' he said.

'Anybody say anything to you today?'

'No.'

'Anybody remark anything peculiar?'

'No. Have you not made tea yet?' He was disgruntled. He was so right to mention it. During tea we had a conversation.

'Did Brutus Iscariot see you?'

'Yes.'

'I had a bloody great spiritual day in the attic.'

'Good, that's the place to be, the attic.'

'I feel marvellous after it, never had to lift my hand all day.'

'There you are, not a tap to do and all day to do it.'

123

'Oh yes, and the peace of it all.'

We had a great conversation like that. I like the bit of company. He offered me the attic for the night. I gladly accepted.

When he came in the following evening, he still bustled about with more copies.

'What's this, I say,' he said, 'no beds made and no tea.' While I did the necessary housework he corrected furiously with my invention. By sheer chance I happened to see one of the copies. 'Good Lord,' I said, 'what are you doing with Rigormortis' copies here?'

'I'm just giving my friend Mr Rigormortis a helping hand,' he answered in a threatening manner.

I went through more of them. 'And Sufferinjaysus and Interruptus? Well I declare, their copies processed by my invention. I'm not at all pleased.'

He looked up at me with that cool cheeky look of his. 'Rest assured that both Quiz school and Quizmasters are indebted to you for your invention.' This had a mollifying effect on me.

That night I had an attic dream; I dreamt that cold porridge was being flung into my eyes. And all the next day uneasy thoughts began to press in on my meditation. I stopped him at the door that evening and checked through his copybooks. My suspicions were correct: he had got to Miss Parnassus. I took his wretched copies and scattered them evenly throughout the house.

'Double crosser,' I roared at him. 'And I thought you were my friend.' I shook the step-ladder in anger. I know I look very terrible in a rage. He crept quietly up into the attic and I pulled the step-ladder away.

'And stay up there from now on. I'm going to work tomorrow.'

He stuck his head down and looked dissatisfied. 'But I must go to work tomorrow or I will be accused of being sick.' I couldn't argue with a man whose face was upside-down.

I was up early, feet washed, shoes polished and all that. I was very pleased as I went into the staff-shed that morning; I like to assert myself. All the Quizmasters were along the wall as usual. Brutus Iscariot detached himself from the noticeboard and came over to me.

'Well, my good man, and what can I do for you?'

'Nothing, I'm going to take my class.'

'You must be mistaken, you are not known here.'

'I'm Anthropos.' There was a dryness in my mouth.

'Where is Mr Anthropos this morning?' he addressed the Quizmasters.

They all surrounded me, their long shadows falling all around me like the spokes of a wheel.

'He must be sick, he's working too hard,' said Sufferin-jaysus.

'Yes, I agree,' yelped Miss Parnassus.

'I'm Anthropos,' I said with the wail of a man betrayed.

'Liar, impostor, actor,' they roared and they pointed their chalky fingers at me. I backed away from these monsters and fled down the steps. I fled along the lanes through the countryside in terror for I felt the shadow of Rigormortis in my rear.

I rushed in the open doorway of my house so fast that I was up the step-ladder and encapsulated in my attic by the man in the rafters before I realized where I was.

'And stay up there,' he shouted after me. 'I'm late already as it is,' and he trotted off to work. I was so jaded from my experience that I never said a word. It took a whole day of meditation for me to regain my composure.

Towards evening as I levitated around the rafters, I heard the screech of metal on stone. Someone was edging a scythe, backwards and forwards went the motion, its sound filling the attic with foreboding. Then I listened in horror to the dry shearing of its blade as it set my plants in a swathe, scattering the green force of their lives on the evening air. I lay back and felt my courage ebb further with each vicious swipe.

He had company in the house. I like company, but this was a woman. I heard their low talk and sudden laughter. The nudges, the knowing winks and the slyness, I could imagine. I groped around the rafters until I found a chink. I put my eye to it. Red hot pokers stabbed my brain; Miss Parnassus was on the sofa. But that wasn't all; flesh, white flesh, the whiteness of sheltered modesty there in carnal display. Oh, the filth of it and the poison of such sinful undertakings. Just anger swept out from my soul and terrible was the sound of my grinding teeth. I'm a terror in a rage. Like Samson I gripped the rafters and could have brought the house down upon their lusting bodies were it not that Mr Anthropos wants no noise from the attic. I lay back and had to listen to their delight while they shared each other's privacy until my sleep released me.

Last night I knocked on the trap-door. After a while he unlocked it and stuck his head up.

'Could I have a drink of water please, sir, it's dry up here.'

He considered this for some time.

'Will you want to make your wee-wee after it?'

'Oh no, sir, that only happens after two drinks of water.'

'Very well,' and he fetched me a nice cool drink.

'I'm rather pleased with your housework, although I would suggest greater effort in the culinary area,' he said.

'Right, sir. You just leave that to me,' I said. 'By the way, sir, when do we have a little chat again? I rather like a little chat.'

He paused to think. 'After tea tomorrow then, if everything is in order.'

I thanked him and he locked the trap-door.

Mr Anthropos is like that, straight if you are straight with him. I help a little now and then but in the attic I am king. Up here I never have to lift a hand, and himself waits on me hand and foot. Up here I have great peace, as I listen to the woodworm burrow the dry seconds of their lives away.

The Wet Eye

IAN COCHRANE

Ma hit me for dirting my face, and I left home straight away. No, that's a lie, I got ready for Sunday school first. But all the time I was getting ready I had it in my head to run away and I did. I never got to Sunday school. Maybe I knew from last week I was going to run away because I hadn't even learnt the verse I was supposed to learn. Anyway it was time I left home because Ma was getting on my nerves. If I wasn't dirty she said it wouldn't be long before I was, and if I *was* dirty then she hit me. She hit me any chance she got. She hit me if I wet my hands, she hit me if I scratched my knee and she hit me if I tried to ride Da's bicycle and got grease on my leg. She hit me too if I threw a bit of bread to the hens, and she hit me if I wasn't feeling too well and couldn't go to school. She hit me if somebody else fought with me or if I cried. She hit me if I ate too much and she hit me if I didn't eat enough. She hit me if I climbed a tree and she hit me if I didn't go out to play. She hit me if I kept quiet because she thought I had done something wrong and she hit me if I was noisy.

When I ran away I went to Uncle Robert's because I knew he wouldn't hit me. I told him about Ma hitting me and he listened. Then he took a big deep breath and never breathed out again for a long time. Then he says, 'You're right.' And then he thought it over for a long time. I just sat there with him in front of the fire and watched him thinking.

After a while he says 'There's one thing you've got to learn.'

'What's that?' I ask.

'Never trust a woman,' he says. I said I would remember that, and that was it settled. I was going to stay with him.

We sat in front of the fire and Uncle chewed tobacco slow and I knew there was something going round in his mind. For a bit I thought maybe he didn't want me, but then he says, 'If

127

you're going to live here, we've got to eat.'

He chewed his tobacco slow for a long time again. Then he says 'We've got to sow the land.'

'What land?' I ask. Because I know that Uncle has no land except for a couple of yards in front of the house and a couple of yards at the back, and it was in pretty bad shape. It was just nettles, briars and stones and a few tin cans and barrel hoops. He looked a bit hurt when I said, 'What land,' and I didn't know what to say.

'My land,' he says. And I said nothing. Then we got started talking about it and I forgot about the size of it. We were going to plant apple trees and plum trees and we were going to keep the hens for the eggs and maybe a cow for the milk. And we were going to plant all sorts of vegetables and everything. We talked and talked about our plans and we went to bed and talked about them. And next morning we got up and we were still talking about them. We talked about our plans until lunch time then we went to the pub and we still talked. Uncle didn't ask me if I drank. He just went up to the bar and came back with two pints. I tasted it and twisted up my face.

'It puts lead in your pencil,' he says. 'It makes your toes open and close with a bang.' Then I drank it slow like him.

'First things first,' he says. And I wondered what he meant. He chewed his tobacco and nearly finished his pint before he said any more. Then he says, 'We need a spade and a hook.'

'Is the hook for clearing the nettles?' I ask him. He looks at me as if I was a genius or something.

'That's right, that's right,' he says.

There's one thing I learnt from Uncle that day. That is not to rush things. I says we better get back and get stuck in, and he just says, 'Never walk before you can crawl.'

'Will we have to buy a spade?' I say.

'We'll cross that bridge when we come to it,' he says. 'I'll have a look in the shed to see what I've got.' Uncle had no idea what he had got in the shed.

That day I only had the one pint. He said it was enough for me to start off with. He had five or six. After he had about three he started to talk about his land again. If there wasn't a spade and a hook in the shed he knew where he could borrow them. It was a chap that drank with him sometimes. Uncle had known him for thirty years. One time he came to Uncle when he had a broken chain on his bicycle and he had to go to a funeral the next day, and even though it was late, Uncle put the chain together and wouldn't take any money for it because he was going to a funeral. The man never forgot about this and every time he saw Uncle Robert in the pub he would buy him a pint. But they never got even because Uncle always bought him one back. So the man told him that if ever he could do anything for him he would. So Uncle told him he might be able to help him some day. Now the time had come.

Uncle said we would have one for the road and we had two and then we went to see the man. We had to walk a long way across the fields. The man lived in a little hut much the same as Uncle's — with a big shed beside it. Uncle forgot to look in his shed and he told the man that if he found out that he had a spade and hook he would bring his straight back. The man was a thin man and his name was James. He smoked a pipe and he had the top of a pepper box stuck over the bowl to keep the ash from falling out. His house smelt of soap and polish. It was cleaner than Uncle's too. Uncle went straight in and told him that he was going to work his little bit of land and James says straight away, 'Well, if there's anything I can do.' And Uncle says, as if he had just thought about it, 'Well, while I'm here, come to think about it, there is.'

Then he told James what he wanted and James went straight out and threw the shed door open and told Uncle to take what he wanted. Uncle says he would only have the spade and hook, and James insisted that he have a shovel too, but Uncle wouldn't hear of it. All he had come for was the spade and hook and he was taking nothing else. They had a bit of an argument about it. Uncle said that he would bring the spade and hook back as soon as he had finished with them, and James said there was no hurry for them and Uncle says that he wouldn't keep anything longer than necessary — that he would be straight over with them on the same day as he had finished, and James says to Uncle that if he didn't stop talking like that he would hit him. Uncle says that if there was one thing he wouldn't do, that is fight with a friend. Uncle says he would rather come to James to borrow something than to a relation. James agreed. He said he never asked a relation for nothing and Uncle said neither did he. Then James insisted that Uncle come in and have a cup of tea. Uncle said no, that he would get back and get started. But it was no good. James pretended to be offended, and Uncle didn't want to hurt him so we had to go in. The kettle was singing on the little black stove and a big black cat was lying curled up on a chair and it was purring loud. Uncle was going to sit down then he saw the cat and he said he would stand. But James wouldn't hear of that. He pushed the cat off the chair and made Uncle sit down. I sat on a little stool. James went down into a little room and back and slipped a round white peppermint into my hand and winked at me as much as to say, not to tell Uncle. Uncle pretended not to see and I slipped it into my mouth.

James kept his pipe in his mouth all the time. Even when he was talking. He had a white shirt on too. It was nice and clean and it had a stud on the neck but no collar. Every now and then he would put his hand up to his neck as if he thought there was a tie there.

Uncle looked all around the room and looked as if he wanted to say something but couldn't think what. Then he looked out the window.

'It's not a bad day,' he says.

'No,' James says, 'it's not. I wouldn't mind if it stayed like this — I wouldn't mind if it stayed like this the whole year round,' Uncle agreed with him, and said that he didn't like it if it was too hot either. James said that he didn't know who was tampering with the weather, but it wasn't as good as it was. You couldn't tell the difference between winter and summer. Uncle said that nature wasn't to be tampered with. Then Uncle went on again about the spade and hook. He would bring it back as soon as he had finished. Uncle never brought anything back he borrowed — he was known for that. Folk said that Uncle would never ask anybody to buy his pint for him but never to lend him anything. Uncle told James about the time he lent a man a hammer and he never brought it back. He said he held nothing against the man, but he would never lend him anything again. Then James told about the time he lent a man a pound and he was a wealthy man, but he never paid it back. After that we set off for home. I carried the hook and Uncle carried the spade. He carried it over his shoulder and he looked just like a man coming home from work.

We were just coming up to Uncle's house when we saw Da standing at the door. We both stopped, but it was too late, Da had seen us.

'You'll not let him take me back,' I say to Uncle.

'Oh, no,' he says and walks straight on with the spade over his shoulder and his chin shot out.

'I can't go back anyway,' I say. 'We have all that work to do. It'll take us a while of getting that land ready.'

Da had one hand in his pocket and he didn't look too upset.

'Do you want something?' Uncle says when we got up to him.

Da didn't answer him. He just looked at me.

'Are you coming or staying?' he says.

'Staying,' I say and he just walks away. He doesn't walk quick — he just walks at his ease. Uncle puts the spade to the ground and leans on it and watches Da walking away. Then when he has gone out of sight Uncle looks at me and takes a big deep breath.

'Do you want to stay or go?' he says.

'Stay,' I say. Uncle brings out his handkerchief and wipes his brow and then looks to see how much sweat is on it.

'That was a near thing,' he says. Then we go and put the hook and spade in the shed and bar the door.

'Are we not going to start on that bit of land?' I say.

'Never run before you can walk,' he says.

We looked at the couple of yards at the front of the house, then we went round and looked at the couple of yards at the back. Then we went inside. Uncle says nothing for a while. He just went down into the bedroom and starts taking off his clothes. I didn't know what to say, so I just started taking off my clothes too. He got into bed and I got

131

in too. We both lay on our backs. Then Uncle groped under the bed and brought out a lemonade bottle full of still. He drank some of the still laying on his back.

The bedroom smelt of cold for a while, then when Uncle had breathed in it for a while it got warmer. And the bed felt warmer too. Uncle was half way down the bottle before he started talking.

'Oh, it's lovely stuff,' he says, and licked his wet lips. Then he starts singing.

> I'm a rambler, I'm a gambler
> I'm a long way from home
> And if you don't like me
> Just leave me alone,
> I'll eat when I'm hungry
> And I'll drink when I'm dry
> And if moonshine don't kill me
> I'll live till I die.

Then he looks at me. 'I used to be a tramp,' he says. I turned round and listened to him.

'Oh, I was. I used to walk the road in the spring mornings. The grass was wet and green, and I didn't have a problem in my mind. I loved the spring sky. I would sing to myself and walk at my leisure. At night I would lie and sing under the sky. In the morning I would be glad to see the new day. And I would thank God that there was no woman to follow me. You can't live with a woman. You can't get on with them. You have to take your own road and leave them behind.'

'I think you're right,' I say.

'I'm right all right,' he says 'I had a woman once. Yes, I met her on my travels. She took me in and fed me and gave me a bed to sleep in. I thought I was happy at first. Then something happened.'

'What?' I ask him. He stuck his leg out of the bed and pointed to his feet.

'Them,' he says. 'I got itchy feet.' He put his leg back into the bed and drank a bit more still. Then he went on, 'I told her that I had to get on the road and she went mad. She shouted at me, she hit me and started tearing her hair out. She pulled it out in big handfuls and threw it on the ground. She stamped her feet till there was no soles in her shoes. She bit her nails till there was nothing left, only little stumps of fingers. She screamed till she burst her ears and she cried like a child.'

'What did you do?' I ask.

'I hit her and left,' he says. 'No, that was the end of that.' Then he looks at me.

'Never get caught,' he says and he closed his eyes and kept on talking. 'In my travels one night I came across a little fire in the dark. I sat down and warmed my feet.' Then there was a loud knock on the door. Uncle opened his eyes and then closed them again.

'Who is it?' he says.

'I'm not sure,' I say and we both lay still. Then the door got another loud bang. Uncle got up slow and went and looked out the window. Then he came back and got into bed. He didn't bother to say who it was and I didn't ask him. The door got another bang and I went to the window. It was Ma. I went and got into bed beside Uncle. Then Ma starts shouting in the door.

'I know you're in,' she shouts, 'I can smell you.'

'That's women for you,' Uncle shouts. 'They can't let sleeping dogs lie.'

'You lazy bugger,' Ma shouts.

'Does she mean you or me?' I say to Uncle. He took a big swig from the bottle and let his lips stay wet and closed his eyes.

'Does it matter,' he says. Ma must have been kicking the door now and she was shouting loud too.

'I'll report you to the authorities,' she shouts. 'You dirty big bugger. You got no right to him. He's only an innocent child. If he would stay at home and go to school and get something into his thick head. He learns nothing. I'll report you. You never were no good. You're a tramp – a dirty tramp. I sent him and he done nothing, but I'll do something. I'll report you. Is there something wrong with your head, or do you just like little boys?' Then she put on a kind of girlish voice. 'Do you just like little boys? Maybe you like little boys better than women. Maybe you need your head examined.' Uncle opened his eyes as if he was surprised that she was still at the door — as if he had been sleeping.

'Go home,' he shouts and closed his eyes again. His lips were still wet from the still. It sounded like Ma had gone. There was no noise for a long time.

'Maybe she won't come back again?' I say.

'If she's away,' Uncle says. Then there was a merciful scream at the window like a wild cat.

'Dirty bugger, dirty bugger,' she shouts. She was scratching at the window like a wild cat too, and her face was screwed up. 'You dirty bugger. Maybe you like little boys. Or maybe you're mad. I'll get you locked up. I'll get the police. A dirty drunkard. You would drink piss.'

Uncle got up in his shirt tails and went to the window and shot out his fist towards her. He didn't touch the glass. She jerked her head away and spat, then ran for all she was worth. I'm not sure whether she ran because Uncle had shot out his fist at her, or maybe it was because she'd seen Uncle with just his shirt on and it short because he had cut off the front to make a handkerchief.

'If you want to go, you can,' he says to me.

'No, I'd rather stay,' I say.

I was happy when I was with Uncle. He had a good heart and Ma was always trying to get him into trouble. One time she told the police that Uncle was walking the roads at night with a big black coat on, and trying to scare young girls. Uncle never did that. He never did it and he never had a big black coat either. And one time she told the Methodist Minister that Uncle jumped out at her when she was coming home from church. And she said he tore the buttons off her coat and she never had no buttons on it in the first place. The Methodist Minister came to see Uncle about that and Uncle just spat on the ground, as if he had just tasted something sour, and slammed the door in his face.

After Ma ran away, Uncle got up and put on his clothes and so did I. He said you got no peace to sleep round here. He said that folk wouldn't leave you alone. He sat in front of the fire with the bottle beside him.

'I never done nobody no harm,' he says and his lip twitched a bit and I thought he was going to cry.

'I know,' I say, and I was near crying too. But it was the drink with Uncle. One of those big bottles and maybe he would dance or maybe he would cry. I seen him crying before and I cried too. One thing about Uncle, he had a good heart.

He finished the bottle and looked at me.

'You're a good boy,' he says. 'You never done me no harm. Not like some folk.' I didn't know what to say. There was a little tear in the corner of my eye and I didn't want him to see it. I turned and looked towards the window.

'I think it's going to rain,' I say. Then I wiped my eye quick.

'Only you and my mother never done me no harm,' he says.

'Everybody likes you,' I say. He put the bottle up to his lips again but there was nothing in it.

'They tried to get me put away one time,' he says. Then he kind of sobs.

'They tried to get me locked up — but I never harmed nobody.'

'I never seen you harm nobody,' I say.

'I pay for my drink and I ask nobody for nothing,' he says. 'They tried to get the doctor to come and certify me but he didn't come. They said I needed treatment, but it's them that need treatment.'

'They all need treatment,' I say. He looks at me with his big mouth open and there were tears in his eyes. But he laughed.

'You're a funny boy,' he says and he came over and ruffled my hair. Then he sat down and put his hand on his brow.

'That's right, son. They all need treatment.' His big head shook and he was crying.

'Dear, sweet mother,' he says, 'you are away from it all now. Maybe I wasn't a good son, but I loved you. Dear old mother dead. You went and left me. I loved you, mother, and there's nobody going to say nothing about you.' I sat and looked at him and not knowing what to do. His big soft head and his big soft heart. His shoulders shook. My eyes got wet again, and I went over and put my arm round his neck.

He put his arm round my waist and we didn't speak for a long time. Then I say, 'Where's she buried?'

'She's dead, son, she's dead,' he says.

'Maybe we could take her some flowers,' I say. He looks at me. His big red face and them eyes wet and the white of them full of little red lines like a map.

'You're right, son,' he says. Then he stands up.

'We'll get flowers,' he says. He went and put a cap on and wiped his eyes with the back of his hand. Then he took out his handkerchief and wipes his nose. You could see his loose lips moving from side to side.

We started off walking through the fields. There was a fine cool rain coming down. It was nice and cool on the eyes. After we crossed the first field, Uncle put his arm round my shoulder and told me that I would get on, that I had a good brain. He walked fast and my legs were moving twice to every one step of his. I tried to take the same steps as him, because I wanted to be the same as him, but it was hard, and after a while I gave up. Then Uncle started talking about his mother again. He said about how she used to make soda bread and he used to eat it fresh from the griddle with butter on it and the butter melting. And she used to make her own butter too and he drank the buttermilk. It was great stuff. In the evenings him and her sat round the fire and she used to throw potatoes in it to bake. She would sing too. She had a voice that would charm the birds off the trees. It came from her soul. She would sing, 'I cursed and I swore at my father, I told him his words were a lie.' It was a sad song, and Uncle sung it to me to let me know what it was like. I could see it all in my mind. I never knew her but I could picture her. She was a fat, cosy woman with grey hair and a dimple on her chin. Uncle was a bit like me, only he still wore the same cap. The big fire and the black potatoes, and Uncle poking them in the fire to see if they were ready. And the house smelling of pipe smoke too. A nice warm, sweet smell. The kitchen was cool and smelt of butter and buttermilk. And sometimes it didn't smell so nice. Sometimes it smelt a bit sour and stale. That was in the morning, just after Uncle got up and the kitchen hadn't started having a nice smell and the big fire was cold.

136

We came out onto a mucky land and Uncle told me to get onto his back, because it was deep and wet, and I had only a thin pair of shoes with holes in them on. He bumped up and down and his boots sucked in the muck. He was still talking about his mother. He has a little red scar on the back of his neck. He must have been hit with something sharp at one time. His neck went up and down as he walked, like a horse. The lane was narrow and the bushes on cither side were almost meeting in the middle, and they were high, too, and wet. But Uncle went straight through them — even the big wet briars that were sticking out. Up near the top there was a honeysuckle and Uncle let go one of my legs and picked a flower. Then when we got to the top he let me down and showed me how to bite the little nipple off the end and suck the honey out.

We walked for a long time before we came to a little new house at the bottom of a good lane. It was built with brick, and it had a thing on the chimney that swayed in the breeze. Uncle explained to me that it was to tell you what way the wind was blowing. I couldn't understand why they wanted to know, and Uncle didn't bother to explain. We didn't walk straight to the house. We went down the lane and into a field, then we went up the side of the ditch towards their back garden. It was full of all sorts of flowers dripping in the fine rain. When we got to the hedge that separated the garden from the field, Uncle signed for me to wait and he bent down and went along the side of the hedge. Then he got down on his hands and knees and disappeared into the hedge. I felt a bit shaky because if folk caught you in their garden they could shoot you. I stood there cold, and shivering every now and then. I stood for a long time. Then I seen the big bunch of flowers coming out the hole first, then Uncle. He had a big grin on his face and he wasn't scared at all. We examined the flowers. They were roses. On the way back Uncle took a long sniff every now and then and he would let me have a good sniff at them too.

The graveyard was grown over. You could hardly see the graves at all. Me and Uncle went straight to one that had no gravestone. There was just one glass wreath on it, and it was almost covered in nettles. Uncle pulled them out with his bare hands and they didn't seem to sting him. Inside the wreath it said, HERE LIES MY MOTHER, MRS PETERSON, BORN 1836, REMEMBERED BY HER SON ROBERT SOLGER. Uncle wasted no time. He just lifted the glass off and stuck the flowers in and walked away. I thought he might have prayed or something even though he didn't believe in praying.

We went home and brought the hook and the spade out of the shed and washed them, then we put them back again. Uncle and me sat in front of the fire. It seemed like we had done a good day's work, and we deserved the rest. Uncle was in a good mood again. He didn't talk about his mother anymore. We got the pan out and made mealy Crushie. It was easy to make. You just fried the meal. But Uncle said it was good for you. He said there was more in one panful of that than there was in a cow. When it got dark Uncle was almost sleeping in front of the fire. He wakened up quickly and looked at the clock as if he had slept or something. Then he couldn't find his cap and he had been sitting on it all the time. After he found it he slowed down a bit. He sat back on the chair and started waking up slowly. He stretched his legs — tried to pull his face into a pucker with his two hands and then he stretched his arms as if he couldn't stretch them far enough.

'I suppose we better go to the pub,' he says.

Ma never let us alone after that day. She was always scrabbling at the window or thumping the door. She said she would see Uncle in hell. Uncle got more and more fed up. Then one day he goes out into the shed and comes back in with a shot gun.

'What's that for?' I ask him. He didn't answer me for a while, and I asked him again.

'You want to stay here,' he says.

'That's right,' I say.

'Then,' he says, 'if you're going to stay here I need some peace. I need no woman bothering me every day. I can do without that.'

'But you can't shoot her,' I say. He didn't answer, but he looked at me as if he was saying, 'Can I not?' Then he started cleaning the gun. It was a double-barrelled gun and he pulled an oily rag through it and looked down the barrels with one eye closed for about an hour. After it was well cleaned he went into a cupboard and brought out a box of cartridges. He slipped two in the gun and closed it up, then he went to the door and I heard the shot. He came back in with a smile on his face as if he had just shot a lion.

'It works,' he says. Then he took the empty cartridge out and threw it into the fire and started cleaning it again. After he had finished this time he put two cartridges in it and went down and put it at the side of the bed. During the night he wakened up several times to make sure the gun was still there.

First thing he did in the morning was to go out and climb up onto the roof with the gun and sit there. I wanted to go up too, but he told me to stay inside. He sat for two or three hours before Ma came. She had the Reverend Carson with her. The Reverend Carson was the same thickness the whole way down and his chin and neck were all in one. It was him that shouted at Uncle first. He didn't see the gun at first.

'You give that boy back to his mother,' he shouts.

'You go home or I'll shoot you,' Uncle shouts and picks up the gun and points it at him. Him and Ma walk slower.

'You need to get locked up,' Ma shouts.

'If you don't go home you'll get locked up in a coffin,' Uncle shouts.

'The man above you is watching you,' the Reverend Carson shouts.

'I don't care,' Uncle shouts. 'You just get home unless you want some lead.'

'You'll suffer for this,' Ma shouts. 'You'll go straight to hell. You'll get jail.'

'One more step and I'll shoot,' Uncle shouts. They both stop dead.

'Come down and talk,' the Reverend Carson shouts.

'Maybe you like little boys,' Ma shouts. 'Maybe that's why you never got married or maybe it was because you were too dirty. When did you last wash?'

'You better go home,' Uncle shouts. 'You take one more step and you'll get the lead pumped into you.'

Then Ma says something to the Reverend Carson and the Reverend Carson shouts, 'I studied law, and I'm here on behalf of this woman and I tell you to let that boy go to his rightful mother.'

'Right,' Uncle says. 'If you stay there, then the boy can go if he wants.' Then he shouts in to me, 'You can go son, if you want to.' I stayed where I was and there was silence for a long time.

Then Uncle shouts, 'There, did he go?' Ma burst out into a temper and her and the Reverend Carson took two or three steps forward.

'Give him back, you dirty bugger,' she shouts, 'You're a filthy bugger, you'll roast in hell.'

'God will punish you for this,' the Reverend Carson was shouting, 'God will smite you.'

'Stop!' Uncle shouts. But they didn't or maybe they didn't hear him. Then there was a bang and they stopped all right.

'Bugger!' Ma shouts. 'Lazy dirty bugger!'

'You take another step and you'll get it this time,' Uncle shouts.

Ma and the Reverend Carson talked amongst themselves for a bit and Uncle just sat there waiting. Then the Reverend Carson takes two big steps forward and there was a bang. Then he was standing there with an ear missing and ma was going away quick and the Reverend Carson was going away quick too. I reckon they never thought Uncle would shoot.

It wasn't long before they were out of sight and Uncle came down from the roof and he didn't talk about it. He went and put the gun in the shed and we talked about the land.

The Miler

BRYAN MacMAHON

'Ave Maria: Guests Welcome,' the sign said. Reading its white letters on a black wooden shield, I smiled: the 'Ave Maria' could well have been an invocation of the Virgin, imploring her to guard the house against incontinent guests.

Leaving the car, I peered down over the fuchsia hedge at the large building that lay below road level and which was now outlined against the evening sea. Obviously a converted barracks or coastguard station, a few faded sycamore trees grew in the lee of its walls, their autumn leaves robbing the stone-work of a little of its austerity. On the hillside to my right a ploughman and a pair of horses had halted at the bottom of a newly-broken field: city bred, I thought late August an odd time of year for a ploughman to be at work.

I am a runner and, at that time, I was training for the Irish mile. Whenever circumstances allowed, I combined my annual holidays with a stint of dedicated training. Thus, that late summer and early autumn, I had driven southward along the west coast of Ireland. Whenever I came upon a stretch of roadway above the sea, I left the car, and pulling off my track suit which I wore over my vest and trunks, jogged for a mile or so away from the car and in the direction from which I had come. Then turning about, I jogged back to the car and, having run a further mile in the direction in which the car was facing, finished with a sharp sprint as again I returned to the vehicle.

This routine I repeated twice, or even three times, during the day. I thought this method of reaching fitness much more interesting than slogging at twilight through the suburbs of Dublin.

I was now in the extreme south-west of Munster — in an area where a dour rampart of cliff was broken only by untenanted coves. The traditional incidence of smuggling together with the folk-memory of a French invasion fleet in

141

the area, must have necessitated, in British days, the building of such a stronghold. In later times, the building, now fallen into disuse, had likely been put up for auction. Still looking at the sign, I reckoned it a brave man — or woman — who had undertaken the conversion of such a fortress to a guesthouse.

Stay there for a night? I pondered the question. 'Ave Maria! Guests welcome,' I repeated to myself as if it were a prayer.

Then came a surprise, for on walking a few yards along the roadway I saw eight or nine motor cars parked under the sycamore trees below. The tourist plates on the vehicles, white, striped and blue, told me that, for the most part, the cars were from the continent.

With a start, I realized that it was the Saturday preceding a bank holiday and that if I did not make up my mind at once I might be forced to spend the night huddled up in the back seat of the car.

I coasted down a driveway between a rout of rhododendrons and grated to a halt under the grey-green stone walls. Above me were the slits of latticed windows with corner turrets set at all sorts of angles, whence, very likely, a view could be had of the sea and the coastline to the north and south.

I left the car and entered the outer whitewashed hall of the guesthouse. I knocked on the black-painted knocker on the inner glass door and waited. The house seemed lifeless.

As I banged on the knocker a second time, a sweet-faced girl, a wing of her black hair sliding across her eyes, opened the door. The smell of good cooking rode out over the smell of stone. The girl looked wide-eyed at me.

'Could I have an evening meal, bed and breakfast?' I asked.

Before the words were fully out of my mouth, 'We're full,' the girl blurted. 'Oh,' I said, 'Could I see the manager?' to be answered all of a rush by, 'There's no one only the missus!' 'The missus?' I repeated and again the girl came full pelt with 'We're full! We're turnin' 'em away all evenin'!'

The girl drew back a little and waited for me to be off.

But I was resolved to try to impose my will on the girl as so often I had tried to impose my will on my rivals in a race. The smell of cooking had sharpened my appetite: the girl, however, seemed determined to shut the door in my face.

I now pretended to yield a point: 'Ask your missus if she would give me a meal,' I said. 'Then if there is still no room I'll push on.'

'I tell you we're full,' the girl repeated. At which I said sternly, 'Please ask your missus!' The girl, a wiggle of fear in her eyes, closed the door and thumped away. I was left alone in the flagstone hall.

With the sound of the sea for company, I waited. After a time I turned and tapped softly with my fingertips on the face of a large barometer hanging on the wall. The needle was falling. I had already found more than a hint of coldness about my shoulder-blades and realized too that I had heard the faint sob of rain in the evening breeze.

The girl re-opened the door; her dilated eyes indicated that I should follow her. An oil lamp, not yet alight, hung from the ceiling of the inner hall.

Entering the dining room, its walls of stone with white-washed edgings on the doors and windows and a candle casting its wan light on each table, the girl glanced at the guests already seated. It was as if she were apologizing for the presence of an intruder dressed in a track-suit. As she made to lead me to a side table which stood in the semi-darkness of an alcove, I enquired for a place in which to wash my hands: this necessitated my following the girl along a corridor and entering an old-fashioned lamplit bathroom in which stood a large bath-tub with the feet of a monster. The water racing into the large hand-basin was almost boiling and the towels were clean.

I returned to the dining room; from the alcove in which I sat I could watch the greater part of the dining room. The guests were mostly continentals — about sixteen or seventeen persons in all. I listened to the low murmur in different languages: German I recognized, Swedish too, and after a time the bird-like peckings of French. As far as I could tell I was the only Irish person present.

The day's exercise had given me a sharp appetite. The meal was a good one. First, onion soup with pot-oven bread and home-made butter followed by boiled salmon with parsley sauce. For main course I had roast lamb with mint sauce and potatoes that were balls of flour — the whole followed by a pleasant dessert of carrageen sea-moss and cream. Finally, I had cheddar cheese, cream crackers and strong black coffee.

My blue track-suit rendering me inconspicuous, I continued to listen to the quiet chatter of the other guests around whom darkness was now gathering. Now and again there was a dull flash of silver in the half light of the room and the faint gurgle of wine being poured. The maid who had opened the door for me served the tables. Once I glimpsed her taking a laden tray of food from hands outstretched from a nearby corridor.

By the time the meal had ended it was dark outside. The maid returned to the dining room, and lighted successively four oil lamps clamped to the walls.

I drew out the end of the meal to the full, gambling on the fact that the later the evening grew the greater was the likelihood of my being allowed to stay. The maid kept casting me an anxious eye, as if telling me to pay my bill and be off. When, in decency, I could delay no longer I stood up and walked towards the door of the dining room. The other guests barely raised their heads to see me go. In the inner hallway, lit now by the overhead oil lamp, the girl, chit in hand, was waiting for me. Groping slowly in my pocket book I asked suddenly, 'Could I see the proprietress?'

'We're full!'

'Could I see her just the same?'

The girl mumbled something and moved through an opening shaped like a Gothic archway. I heard the put-put of heavy raindrops falling on the gravel outside.

'Yes?'

I turned. A youngish woman, a little flushed, obviously as a result of cooking the meal, was standing before me. The lamp was directly above my head, so that for a moment or two I could not help noting the restrained vividness of her face. I had a sense of seeing remotely her well-tapered legs. 'Thank you for a pleasant meal,' I began; then 'Could you put me up for the night? I'm not particular where I sleep.'

Adroitly the woman had moved around me until the light was falling fully on my face and body. She glanced with interest at my track-suit. 'Every room is full,' she said a little hesitantly and in a musical voice, 'but if you drive on twenty-five miles you may . . .'

'I've slept rough before,' I told her, now holding the five-pound note in my hand. Risking a laugh, I added, 'I'm strong and healthy.'

The woman looked from the note to my face, then paused to listen to the roar of a thunder shower on the gravel outside. Again she looked at me. Rather hesitantly, she began, 'If you wouldn't mind sharing a room . . .'

'Not at all!'

There was a pause, in which the woman again looked at me carefully.

'It's difficult to explain,' she said quietly. 'Your room-mate is old. He's a priest. Rather nervy, too. He won't bother you though. He'll come in late and will be gone before you wake up in the morning. Whatever happens you mustn't disturb him.'

'I'll be careful,' I said.

'Very well!'

The woman turned; taking a lighted candle from a table in a nearby passageway, she led the way up a flight of pine stairs, along a corridor, then up a second flight of stairs. At last she led me to a rather small strongly made door, which, when opened, showed a step down into a bedroom.

Entering at her heels I saw that the place seemed larger that it really was — this possibly because of the fact that the floor of the room was on three levels. One was the level on which we stood, on the left of which was a narrow divan bed; in one corner diagonally opposite the door and a step up was a recess in a turret, obviously a place designed for the observation of the sea below. The third level was reached by a step down into a wall embrasure. This last held a spacious low-slung bed with a dark curtain half-drawn across the front of it. The bed filled almost all the space in the embrasure.

The room as a whole seemed medievally intimate: the furniture of dark mahogany showed up starkly against the plastered white walls. The place also had a stage unity which was enhanced by the shifting candlelight. In a wall-niche was a statue of the Virgin in coloured wood — Bavarian, I guessed.

Superimposed on the remote smell of unusedness that hung about the place was another smell I could neither isolate nor define — it could well have been incense — that is if the priest were not retired or silenced. On the edge of the range of the candle flame I noticed a square mirror which I recognized as French, and on a slender-legged table beneath it, a graceful blue jug and water ewer, the neck and handle of the ewer suggesting a sailing swan. The narrow divan was not made up: this bed was clearly meant for me and the bed in the embrasure was where the priest slept. 'I'll have it made up for you at once,' the woman said with reference to the divan. She indicated an old-fashioned candle sconce with a box of matches in it, then added, 'You will need somewhere to change.'

I murmured my acceptance of the room and my thanks. We went downstairs. Taking my overnight bag and suit from the boot of the car I had a bath — rather belatedly now that the meal was over, I told myself, and then putting on my tweed suit went for a stroll before going to bed.

The shower had ended. The evening air smelled of autumn. There was a fitful moon. I could see the outlines of a pier dark against the silver of sea water, so I headed downwards along a pathway that led towards it. At the pier-head a hunched-up old man stood looking out onto the water. I stood beside him. Above us was a huge boulder cloven as by an enormous axe; moving a few steps so that the rock no longer obscured my view I saw a cluster of lights — obviously a village on yet another peninsula.

After we had exchanged a few words on the weather, the old man absent-mindedly told me the legend of a giant splitting the rock, and then said, 'I'm watching the seals!'

I then saw what I took to be a seal swimming in the moon glitter of the sea. 'May Christ sweep you off the face of the map!' the old man shouted. 'You have all my salmon carried.' At the sound of the raised voice the seal seemed to tread water. For a while its sagacious head was turned in our direction.

'Dangerous bastards!' the old fellow went on. 'They

146

attacked me one day in a cave.' He pointed to a cliffside. 'In there on a flat rock they couple, face to face — like man and woman!'

We lapsed into a companionable silence. Far to the north a lighthouse blinked intermittently. After a time three tinker girls appeared, seemingly out of nowhere: two of the three used the third, who appeared to be a simpleton, as a foil. All three indicated wantonness in the manner in which they begged for money and in the violent way in which they pushed one another when they were near us. The foolish one — she could have been eighteen — as a result of one such a push cannoned off me so that I had to catch her before she went sprawling. I shall not readily forget the contrast between her ripe vital body and the idiocy of her face. As, for a moment, I held her close to me, she seemed to be struggling up to some novel kind of understanding. It was a fleeting, but for me an illuminating, moment. Then the old man beside me raised his stick and all three ran off screaming into the darkness.

As a result of our shared indignation — his real enough, mine simulated, the old man and I were now a little closer. 'You're staying up above?' he asked, indicating the bulk of the guesthouse. On my admitting that I was, I began to question him. According to him, the woman (he called her a girl) who owned the place was from the Irish midlands: she had either been a novice nun or a student nurse (or both) in England and had married a wealthy man (one of her first patients) much older than she was. Returning to Ireland the pair had bought the old building, renovated it, and opened it as a guesthouse. The husband had died after a heart attack — he was raising a capstone for a gate-pier when he collapsed; this summer, helped by a girl from the orphanage, the young widow was trying to make a go of the place.

'The troubles in the North aren't helping her one bit,' the old fellow said and then, without a trace of malice towards me, added, 'You'd want to be stone mad, or from Europe itself, to come here at all! And madder still to stop here — even for a night!' As I laughed, 'But give the lassie above her due,' he went on, 'she's a trier! She'd do anything to earn a shilling. But she doesn't mix nor meddle with anyone

147

hereabouts. Nor we with her!'

'Who is the priest?' I asked suddenly.

'What priest?' the old fellow snapped.

'Isn't there a priest staying there?' I asked lightly.

'The Pope of Rome could be staying there for all I know,' the old man said. Then we dropped the subject.

Across the bay a pair of moving parallels of light indicated the progress of a motor car. The old man and I walked together to the gateway to the guesthouse: there we parted. 'Ave Maria. Guests Welcome!' I could barely make out the legend in the darkness.

The house seemed asleep. It was as if the ranked cars resented the sound of my footsteps on the gravel. I turned the black knob on the white door and went in. The wall lamp in the inner hall, its lighting wick turned down, showed me my way to the foot of the stairs. The stairs itself was a sounding box: twice I knocked my toecap loudly against one of the risers. Mercifully there were no creaks.

Half way up, I thought I heard a noise below. I stopped and had a vague sense of someone stealing out to verify that I had returned. Reaching my room, I groped forward to the table on which the candle sconce lay, drew a match against the side of the matchbox and set the flame to the wick. The smell of wax, sulphur, dampness, sea air, and the remote odour that could have been incense — or fresh yeast — touched my nostrils. My watch told me that it was twenty past eleven.

Was the priest a drunkard? I asked myself glancing at the empty bed in the alcove. Or was he one for whom the weight of the priesthood had proved too great a burden? Or was he, like so many of his fellow priests, woman-troubled? Whatever menace hung above him, he seemed to have avoided a climax by holing up like a frightened animal.

Standing in the turret I looked out over the black clumps of rhododendron, over the face of sea, past the cliffside pitted with seals' caves, past the cloven rock to the cluster of lights on the far shore. I remained there watching a lighthouse, once, twice, three times, splay its beam. Then I saw the seascape revert to utter darkness.

Tired after the day, I took off my clothes: standing in mid-floor, one ear turned towards the doorway, I flexed and exercised my naked body for a time. Then I pulled on my pyjamas and lay on the divan bed. Stretching myself with my fingers interlocked about my poll I looked up at the ceiling.

Had I pushed myself too far that day? Had I carried over into the act of driving the tension of my roadwork — that never-ending grind of pushing my body closer to the ultimate boundary of its abilities? I rejected the idea. Last year, I reflected, I had missed winning the senior mile by a yard: this year, if the sports writers were to be believed, O'Connell, the man who had beaten me then, was on the down grade. I was now being hailed as the new champion — 'a certain eratic brilliance notwithstanding', one of the journalists had written about me, using a phrase that kept recurring to me. This year, by Christ, I told myself, God willing or even with the devil's luck, I would beat O'Connell! And any others like O'Connell who thought they could run the mile. After that, national representation was open to me, followed possibly by an athletic scholarship to the United States. Names of places such as Tokyo, Hawaii, Auckland and Helsinki, loomed up before me — I even saw myself on the Olympic team. All this if only I got the initial break of beating O'Connell.

Again, the other side of my mind began to address my taut body telling it that it would be more contented lolling on a beach in Spain or France with a full-bosomed girl touching my shoulder-blades with fingertips that invited without pretending to do so. Why do you have to endure such a harsh discipline, to deny yourself so many luxuries? Do you always have to treat your trunk and limbs as instruments — as appendages to be viewed objectively, never subjectively?

I sighed: for the last five of my twenty-two years, ever since I had won the event in the National Colleges Championships, I had been obsessed by the idea of winning the senior mile. While my sisters and brothers, who referred to me mockingly as 'The Miler', danced and drank, I was always living under the tyranny of the stop-watch.

In the wan light of the bedroom I looked across at the priest's bed: perhaps he too had disciplined himself over-severely, until the system that controlled his nerves had sheered off track. Drawing in air slowly through my nostrils I tried to determine the physical appearance of the man. Fat or thin? Shivery or steady? Morose or loquacious? Sane or downright crazy?

The smell told me nothing. The broad monastic bed in the alcove was altar linen clean: I found myself tempted to rise and touch the priestly pillow and the clean blue coverlet: I did not do so for I feared that with the fine attunement of his senses, the priest might know that I had touched a part of him he held sacramental. 'Who's been sleeping in my bed?' I found myself mimicking Baby Bear in the nursery story.

I blew out the candle flame. For a few moments, a spark on the wick trailed acrid smoke into the air of the room.

The divan was pleasantly hard: I rolled over on one side, turning my face to the wall. I recalled the ploughman now probably as pleasantly tired as I was and the old man on the pier cursing the breeding seals, smiled wryly at the recollection of the trio of wanton tinker girls and finally sent my thoughts over the cloven stone and over the sea to reach the light cluster on the far shore. Invariably a sound sleeper, I soon drifted into sleep.

Asleep and yet not fully so, I heard the priest enter the room. A lightly-built man if I read his movements accurately. A non-smoker, too, my keen sense of smell told me; on drowsy balance my mind was slow to rise consciously to the occasion so that I set aside the temptation to read other clues that came and went on the air of the bedroom. No whiskey though, of that I was sure. Soap, such as I had used myself — he must have taken a late bath and — no smell of incense! I probed no more. Subconsciously I continued to sift him, and found neither enmity nor peril connected with him. I recorded a vague sense of inevitability about his coming as he moved lightly across the floor and stepped down to where his bed was. I heard him rise to tip-toe to draw across the curtain and vaguely considered that while he slept he would be no more than seven or eight feet from me; much more remotely I wondered if he snored. Again I heard the curtain rings bunch, stop, and ever so lightly creak across. After that, a last spark of my consciousness attempted vainly to interpret the various sounds of his clothes as he removed them: I should, by right, hear the muted crackle of his clerical collar and the rustle of the stock being folded in his hands. Too sleepy to sift the sounds further I moved gently downwards into sleep.

After a time (an hour? two hours?) I woke. My shoulder-blades felt cold. Groping, I found that the light upper quilt had slid to the floor. I heaved over and groped about on the floor to find it, at the same time being careful to make no sound that would disturb my room-mate. And then, as I twisted on the bed, the cramp struck!

Struck? Jesus! It did far more than that! It zipped open the muscle of my right thigh, gripped whatever was sinewy between its iron fingertips, tied a single knot in the thigh-string, pulled the ends tight and then zipped up the muscle again. The pain left me struggling, gasping, stretching, extending, butting, clawing, choking back obscenities, sweating, attempting to grip my thigh and later, when I dared to move, pummelling the bunched flesh. And just when I thought the agony had eased, a second cramp unzipped the flesh of my other thigh, knotted up the thong of it and again zipped up the muscle. I blubbered, gibbered, extended both my legs to their full length in a vain effort to find relief by bracing the balls of my toes against the non-existent end of divan. I had difficulty in restraining from screaming.

At last, as both cramps, having apparently passed the high point of their devilishness, eased for a moment, I gathered the bedclothes around my body, rolled off the bed and onto the floor and lay there gasping and grovelling as though I were emerging from an epileptic fit. For a moment or two the twin pains seemed static: it was as if the ferrule of an umbrella had been driven deep into the muscle of each of my thighs. Sweating profusely, for a moment or two I lay without movement. Then I squirmed sidelong across the space that separated the priest's bed from mine. As I moved the double cramp reached a new peak of agony. I clawed at the flimsy curtain so that the brass rod above became dislodged and fell down, striking me on the shoulder before it clattered to the floor.

'Father! Father!' I called. There was no sound from the bed beside me. Something told me that the priest was lying

151

on his back staring up at the ceiling.

Stiffening my legs to the uttermost, and contorted with pain and anger, I raised myself onto my elbow and by a prodigious effort, flung my arm across the priest's body. As I did so, my clawing fingers met the firm breasts of a woman.

The urgency of the pain in my underthighs more than offset my sense of shock at the discovery, so that once again my legs became rigid as they tried to outwit their tormentors. Stretch, stretch, stretch, lie doggo: ebb — ebb! you pair of demons, I blubbered incoherently, as the knots grew less tight. Terrified even to stir lest the cramps return to plague me, I lay there in ebbing agony.

At last . . . At last . . . At last. A-a-ah! The demons were departing.

Exhausted but relieved, still swathed in bedclothes and with the curtain hanging awry across my body, I lay on the floor beside the bed. 'Mm,' I murmured sleepily. Dreamily I pulled the curtain and its entangled rod about my shoulders. The rod clanged a little on being shifted. Breathing deeply I revelled in my release and soon fell asleep.

I do not know how long I slept. Opening my eyes I saw the first grey of day outside the slit of the turret window. A gust of wind rumbled up from the sea and flung harsh raindrops against the glass. I was now fully awake. My fingers, clutching as of their own accord, suddenly remembered.

I came carefully to my knees and looked down at the form in the bed below me. It seemed to lie in a foetal crouch; its face turned to the stone wall and the outer part of the bed offering me room. I paused for a full minute; then, a full-blooded shower urging me on, I raised the bedclothes and moved languorously in until my body came to where the bed had the warmth of an animal's lair. There I drew the bedcovers up about my shoulders. At first, I kept my body a little away from the woman but later, studying every move before I made it, inch by inch I came closer. At last, I lay in a hoop directly behind and against her. Seeking a signal from her body I waited for a long time before making my next move.

152

At last she uttered a barely audible 'Mm' and backed the minutest fraction towards me. I knew then that I was welcome.

Then began the ritual of pleasure-movement that resembled the fidgets of an athlete before the start of a race. At first each movement was the refinement of delicacy for I never knew the moment when the woman would spring up and flounce out of the room. But then I found that my sense of timing, born of the racing mile, now stood me in good stead. In my mind I went over the tactics demanded by the gun-lap, by the second lap and with a sense of zest looked forward to the task of knitting two good minutes to two minutes that were not so good. Experiencing something close to ecstasy I anticipated the moment when the bell would ring for the final lap and the advent of the end, the ultimate sprint that would lead to victory — or defeat.

As I raced this novel mile images came and went in my mind. At one moment sea-water seemed to swirl about the flat rock, on which I, a grey bull seal, wrestled face to face with a young seal cow. Again, on a shift of fancy, I became the bright axe-head poised above the boulder, about to strike down into rock as did the giant of legend in the long ago. Yet again, I was the ploughman on the hill flank, my ploughshare ripping open the warm clay that faced the south and the sun. Again I held the live body of the idiot tinker girl in my arms: I even became the sinning priest of fiction, daring to break his vow of chastity and being broken himself thereby. But having taken these various roles, I reverted inevitably to being the miler, now running in the consummate certainty of victory and welcoming the sweat flowing down over my racing body. All the while I was acutely conscious that my imagination was affording me novel angles of vision on my actions so that my ecstasy was multiplied as would a sensual act executed in a hall of mirrors.

The bell rang for the final lap. By now the woman had become my single remaining opponent. Long since it was as if we two had outdistanced the field. For the first time in my racing career I realized that my body and my imagination were working in harmony: my rival raced as if conveying the certainty that she would breast the tape before I did; I imagined I saw on her constricted face a mocking smile that told me that once again I would become the ever-gallant second, the always-to-be-pitied, the invertedly cherished of the commentators. But as we continued to race shoulder to shoulder I was again taken by the notion that the certainty of victory she appeared to convey was counterfeit and that, with rarest intuition, she was simulating this certainty so as to draw out the last ounce of my resources and ensure that no shred of strength would remain unused in my body or mind after we had finished the race.

As we rounded the last curve the roar of a thunder shower and the sound of the sea became the applause of a great crowd. I was acutely conscious of her limbs moving to a racing rhythm I found exhilarating beyond utterance and one that complemented me fully. The woman was giving to the last yards of the race all the physical and imaginative resources she possessed so that with the finishing line drawing ever nearer, she even dared to inch a little ahead of me. But my shoulder persisted in clinging close to hers and in the final few yards when it seemed that I was beaten, I gathered the remnants of my frenzy, passed her by the narrowest of margins, hurled myself fully forward and flung my body, and indeed my mind, upon the line. Utterly spent, we collapsed, each on the other; as I gasped out to comfort her in defeat, by the quarter light of morning I read in her wet eyes the implication that she construed her defeat as victory. For me, completely drained, on the edge of my consciousness there came and went the flickering images of the coupled seals, the deep-fallen axe, the ploughshare driven into the final furrow, the idiot features of the tinker girl and even the haggard face of the non-existent priest.

In the morning when I awoke, I found myself alone on the bed. I pulled on my track-suit, and later, having washed myself, went down to a breakfast of porridge, strong rashers, a large fried egg with the flavour of the sea in it, wholemeal bread and crab-apple jelly. Of the mistress there was no sign. I paid the waitress my account, thumped my bag into the boot of the car, took the wheel and backing crunchingly on the gravel, halted for a moment to look up at the windows of the building. Gravel spurted from my tyres as I drove towards the roadway above. I stopped my car beside the fence where, firm amid the fuchsia, stood the sign 'Ave Maria! Guests Welcome.'

'Why?' I asked myself. 'For money? For pity? For release? For whim? For season? For no reason and for all reason? Why?'

Above my head the notice board remained inscrutable: if it had been endowed with a voice it probably would have said 'Such a foolish question!' With a final glance at the pier, a stare at the cliff and the cloven rock, a squint at the ploughed field and a wryly muttered 'Mea culpa', I drove away.

As I journeyed to the east, keeping the rampart of cliff on my right hand, I knew that whenever in the years that lay before me I heard the bell ringing for the final lap of the mile, this woman would always be beside me, racing fluently on her tapered legs. And that inexorably I would wear her down, yard by yard, inch by inch, until with a final body-thrust I would breast the tapes just ahead of her.

I also realized that this was the image that had hitherto been missing from my racing life: thus it was with a sense of elation I drove eastward eager to find a suitable stretch of road where I could race and race and race, spurting towards the end in such a manner as indicated the clear certainty of future victories.

Separate Ways

MAURA TREACY

'You're packing early enough, anyway,' May said.

Beega jumped. Later on she wondered why she hadn't noticed the smell of peppermints in time.

'Well, it's easier to do it now than in the morning or when I come in tonight.'

'If you left it too late you might have to stay here another day.'

'There wouldn't be anything wrong with that,' Beega said as convincingly as she could.

'No?' May enquired as she closed the door and wandered across to the window. Outside on the landing another door closed and they heard the preoccupied voices of guests going downstairs to dinner, parting on the stairs to let through a latecomer, exchanging greetings with the uncommitted familiarity of people who've seen each other at meals every day for a week, or at times with the over-reaching friendliness of someone who wanted every acquaintance to be significant and unforgettable.

'Of course not. Anyway you're going to need the room. Leo says you're booked out for the rest of the month.'

'And Leo is the one who knows.' She slung sulkily across the room, her exercise sandals slapping her heels.

Beega knelt down to lock the suitcase on the floor. She fumbled with the key. 'I don't think it's good for you to wear those sandals while you're expecting,' she said, because of all the things she had been itching to say and hoped she could refrain from saying in the short time they were together, that seemed to have the least potential for damage.

'Anything else I'm doing wrong?' May snapped as if she had waited for days, sensing everything that Beega noted and disapproved of, deliberately not correcting anything until Beega would be goaded to a pitch of irritation she couldn't control. Then she'd abandon the awful spinsterish deference she seemed to feel she owed her since May's precipitate marriage had disrupted the co-ordinated progress of their lives. Beega looked at her defiant, waiting face and saw all the familiar signs she hadn't known she remembered. She had begun to hum unconvincingly under her breath and tried to stop it when she recalled that years ago May had asked her if that was her ladylike way of whistling in the dark. Briskly she swept the rest of her clothes one by one off the chair, folded them and stacked them in the open case on the bed. But she was still humming.

May fingered the clothes in the case beside her and unfolded with one hand a pair of hipster slacks. 'Well for you, you can wear clothes like that,' she said and cast them aside.

'You never liked them anyway,' Beega said, retrieving them and packing them again. She locked the case and swung it onto the floor beside the other.

May dipped again into her pocketful of peppermints. 'Have one?'

'I've just brushed my teeth.' She opened her bag and pushed back the curtain for light to see her make-up. 'What are you doing for the rest of the night?' She asked at random because she couldn't bear to have them both concentrating solely on her face. When there was no answer, she held the mirror aside and glanced at May. 'Hm?'

With glacial malice May stared at her, her eyebrows lifted, begging her to suggest, honestly, just what she might find to do in such a place. She mooned around the house most of the day in her nightdress, with her long dressing gown open and floating behind her as she plied dreamily between the box of peppermints on the sideboard, a magazine on a table, a bowl of flowers on the windowsill, the mirror over the mantelpiece. Mostly the guests were out of the house all day fishing, or sometimes Leo led a party of them up into the mountains, and when they were near the end of their stay they would go out sight-seeing and shopping. They went to bed at nine or ten o'clock every night just when May thought the day should be starting, and in the mornings they were up again at six, hours before May would even consider sitting up in bed to eat the breakfast which one of the girls would bring up to her from the kitchen. Eventually she would get up and wander downstairs where there was still nothing for her to do that wasn't already being done adequately since long before she had ever come there.

Sometimes if she saw a new duster in use she would take it and go around flicking it over the backs of chairs, a task she immediately felt disinclined to continue; she'd peel back the corner of a handkerchief or scarf bundled in a corner and find it full of odd shaped and coloured stones or shells; she'd open a tin on the hall-stand and touch with dismal uninterest the peacock colourful flies; as she skirted a corner she'd remember to pluck aside the hem of her dressing gown, but there was nothing there to distress her anymore: the cans of live bait which in her early and brief enthusiasm as chatelaine she had upset, and which had spilled on the floor while she stood screeching as they squirmed and wriggled at her feet had, with all the rods and reels, been banned for her safety and peace of mind to an outhouse. But with their equipment had gone all the company. In the evenings after dinner they used to sit around the fire with Leo for an hour or two until bedtime, at ease in the uncomplicated ambience of bachelorhood, talking of the way they had passed the day. Now in May's burgeoning presence they felt vaguely ashamed of their celibate obsessions and sat outside on the steps or went to their own rooms and wrote to their wives.

'Where are you going now?' she asked Beega, as if her sister's plans were bound to exclude her.

'Into the town. I have to ring Tom, let him know what time I'll be back tomorrow.'

'Doesn't he know that?' May said, looking as all married women eventually did when they came to realize that such considerate attentions were a poor investment. But neither did she wish to encourage Beega to retain her sovereign independence now that she had lost her own. 'Anyway, you could ring from downstairs.'

'I'd rather ring from the town.'

'More private?'

'Yes,' Beega said emphatically, implying that it was an observance that might with benefit be more widespread.

'Ooooh,' May said, 'touchy.'

158

'Get your coat and we'll go.'

'I'm not going.'

'But why? Ah, come on, it's my last night.'

'But not mine, is it.'

They stared at each other. May felt she had a lot of ground to make up. She had been elaborately and imaginatively hospitable at first — she had been so glad to see Beega again — and had set out wholeheartedly to enjoy the time she was there. It was near the end, when she realized that Beega had only a few days left and was already packing away clothes she wouldn't be wearing again, that she saw her mistake. She had shown Beega a lifestyle of leisure and comfort and optional activity, of picturesque health and freedom in the open air, and for nights the vivid life of a tourist centre twenty miles away. It was just the kind of impression that would appeal to Beega and send her home with fulsome ideas of May's contentment. And to crown it all she seemed to regard Leo with a kind of reverent fascination.

'If you'd drive the car you could go when and where you liked.'

But May refused to drive as if any show of self-reliance might weaken her plea of intolerable privation.

'I've had enough driving for today,' she said. And because she knew that her grievances and excuses didn't stand up to unsympathetic examination, she added, unarguably, 'I'm tired.'

When Beega returned, hours after, the house was in darkness save for a glimmer of light in the front room, and as she crossed the gravel the drone and murmur of the men's voices came to her through the open windows. A chair scraped across the floor as it was pushed back. Somebody was going to bed. She heard the sudden effort of the torpid voices bidding him goodnight and she waited outside so as not to prolong the leavetaking.

They were sprawled in the chairs, stupefied with tiredness after the exertions of the day in the open air, dinner in the evening and afterwards the illicit whiskey to which Leo alone reacted positively. Through the open doorway he saw her as she crossed the hallway to the stairs.

'Come on in,' he called, holding out his hand which

nevertheless fell limply down by the chair while he waited for her. The idea charmed her but she had already heard the resentful plodding of May's feet across the landing from the bathroom. Still she went to the door to see who was with him. Two of the men stood up then and shyly said goodnight as they passed by her and went upstairs. Only Paul, a Frenchman who came every year and was on easier terms with the family — which, she was startled to realize, included her — stayed on.

'Well, where did you go this evening?' Leo enquired, the way her mother's friends years ago might have asked: What did you learn in school today? Though not quite the same, she recognized, as she rubbed her aching neck inside her upturned collar and leaned against the jamb of the door. She stared with wonder and weariness into the shadowy room. She was conscious too of the visitors asleep upstairs, a dozen or more of them restoring their healthy minds and the healthy bodies to accommodate them. Leo was drowsy but ready to stir himself if she had anything to tell him. He was watching her and she gave him a reluctant, resentful half-smile. When he was like that, being sociable and friendly and with an uncertain particle of a smile frozen on his lips as if he were going through a routine he had been taught and didn't believe in, it was almost as if he wished indeed that he could feel the kind of interest people often had in the minutiae of each other's lives.

She told him the hotel she had been in. She was faintly embarrassed; it seemed to her that he hardly approved of her mixing two kinds of holiday, and he was intrigued to know why she couldn't take the country as it was without resorting to the popular tourist zone of souvenirs and postcards and bland hotels. She had spent the evening in one, sitting alone in the corner of the lounge, her finger freezing on the rim of a glass, monitoring her own sobriety as she cushioned each glass of vodka on a glass of pineapple.

'I'd better go up and see May,' she said.

'I suppose it's near time we all went,' he said. 'What time is it?' With considerable, yet not enough effort he arched his neck to see the clock on the wall above his chair.

'It's gone twelve.'

160

'Gone twelve,' he murmured as he gazed in wonder into the fire. He crouched forward, holding the glass in his hands between his knees, and slowly shook his head. Some mystery that had always puzzled him had begun to haunt him again lately, and he was no more married now nor less solitary than he had been over a year ago when they had first met him, and she knew now how little she would have injured him by making the very suggestion that had been forcing itself on her and she had been fanatically avoiding – that May should return home. Even when he had been seeing May twice and three times a day in the short time he had known her, he had no real conviction that, even if she did marry him, she would ever stay with him. And now, in so far as he cared at all about other people's opinion, he felt a vague hangover of embarrassment for the inappropriateness of it all: that after a term, the duration of which he had no way of knowing, but which May was already allotting with haphazard instinct, she would leave him.

'I've never seen anything like it,' the forgotten and forgetful Frenchman was musing wistfully, and it was the foreign tinge of his accent that made Beega look at him with mothering, dolorous eyes.

'Aye,' Leo said, 'if he had been ready for it . . .' and his voice sighed away into the silence of the night.

The room was dimly lit with two electric candles above the mantelpiece and the wavering flames of the fire; and shadows swirled and loomed and toppled on the walls around them. Two pairs of canvas shoes were drying on the hearth; the dog was asleep behind a chair and sometimes when he was disturbed he thumped his tail against the door of the dresser behind him.

'Won't you have some?' Leo said eventually, waving towards the bottle.

Without considering the reasons she had always had for declining, she took up a glass off the tray and walked across the room, picking her steps over the Frenchman's feet – later, with bleary recollection of courteousness, he drew them back. She poured half a glassful from the unlabelled bottle and resting on the arm of a chair, she too stared at some random focus. In the flickering smoky dimness they listened to the sedgy silence of the night outside on the wasteland that spread out to where the sea crept up on it, insinuating itself into the weak points, making inroads, isolating small islets that were demolished until nothing was left but a jag of rock and sometimes in a crevice a clump of rough grass that craved landward in the wind when the tide was low.

She yawned deeply, trying not to open her mouth, and in anguish she pressed her face into her hand and said, Oh, Lord, and slowly swung her head to loosen the tiredness of her neck and shoulders. She clutched the glass and drank. Her head soared gently, split open and the stars showered down into the swarming well of her mind. She held her breath and bit by bit the parts of her head reassembled and everything — and eventually the roof of her mouth too — slid back into place.

The dog was thirteen years old. She sat into the chair and peered down over the side of it at him. He couldn't live much longer, though one wet night last summer, on their first visit, when they were all sitting around the room, a German vet had caught the dog's head and looked at its eyes and teeth and then turned him over on his back on the floor, embarrassing them all with his further examination before saying he had seen one live for eighteen years. It was a great age — for a dog — everyone wanted to comment and was lost when somebody else said it first, because then there was nothing else they could think of to say. They just had to stare at the dog with the homage that was expected for him, and try to look impressed and full of thought about the relativity of age between man and animal, until the dog himself padded blindly away between the chairs and released them.

Somewhere and sometime in the night, Leo said, 'Will I top that up for you?' and because she was yawning again she put her hand over the glass. The Frenchman had put down his glass and his head was almost touching the floor as he bent forward in his chair and looked back under it for his shoes. He wore grey socks, and as she stared at them, though her eyes were streaming, she felt as disappointed as if she had met the Shah of Persia in a peaked cap. Before he went up to bed he said goodnight in a stiff formal way that always left

162

her puzzled for a while, he was so friendly all the rest of the day.

'I suppose I'd better go too,' she said, though it might have been an hour later.

'He's a fine chap, Paul,' Leo said in the tired droning voice that reminded her sometimes of bees in an orchard and then again of an Anglo-Irish clergyman's funereal voice saying: 'Thy will be done.'

'He comes back every year,' he added, as if such friendship sustained him but left him unconsoled.

One last half-solid piece of coal was poised on a pile of clinker that dimmed gradually and cracked; Leo touched it in time with the side of his shoe and knocked it back into the diminished heart of the fire where the last flames swarmed around to consume it and when she noticed it again it was reduced to a cinder and the whole fire was dead except for the distant winking of a spark here and there.

'I got iron tablets for May in the chemist's,' she said once when she had counted the ticking of the clock to eighty-nine and she heard the two semi-circular plinks of the bottle as he left it on the table. 'Good,' he said, and after a while he asked, 'Do you think she needs them?' And later on she said, 'They won't do her any harm, anyway.' And still later he agreed, 'No, that's true.' And so their minds drifted, touching at one point of conversation, then diverging in separate paths but circling back eventually to the one tangential point.

May was asleep, lying back against three pillows. Beega left the tablets on the dressing table and began listlessly from habit to rearrange the bottles and jars and jewellery that were jumbled there and the clothes scattered on an armchair and spilling onto the floor; but there were odds and ends belonging to Leo among them and she shied away from them, switched May's slippers into a marginally tidier position before leaving the room. Downstairs Leo was in the kitchen, packing lunches for the next day.

'If you'd let May do all that,' she had said, 'she mightn't have so much time to be discontented.'

'I don't think she'd want to,' he said, and she was relieved and reproved when he left it at that.

Though she would grow used to him and learn to perceive

and understand him beyond all the careless assumptions of familiarity, there would always be an echo of wonder at the way he re-emerged to carry on the routine of his days, since effort hardly seemed possible without optimism.

Honeymoon

JOHN JORDAN

'Thank God,' said Laura to Jo-Jo who had come to her side to stand there like a famished madonna. 'Lottie's tight and father's tight and if we stay any longer Tony and I will be tight and we'll miss the plane.'

Jo-Jo leaned down to Laura's upturned head and kissed her. A little after Laura went to her room to change, and her father, maudlin by this time, slobbered a little on Jo-Jo's shoulder. But she had alchemized her grief into fury at some as yet undefined person or object, and Laura's father found no comfort.

As Laura came to the staircase, Jo-Jo went to her again and spoke to her. Her body looped and strained in her long black dress, and Laura's face was shadowed when she came down into the hall. It was time to go.

Laura and Tony were to be driven alone to the airport, where they were to be flown straight to Paris. Everybody was agreed that the wedding breakfast was a great success. 'A credit to poor Auntie Jo-Jo,' as Laura's father had said. Jo-Jo had shown untypical tact and ingenuity in pairing off guests. For Laura the crown of Jo-Jo's achievement had been the coupling-off of Herbert and Lottie, two survivals from Tony's and Laura's college days. Herbert was a Gold Coast negro who had studied Medicine in Tony's time, and Lottie had been an extravagantly unsuccessful student of Modern Languages while Laura was distinguishing herself. By dint of regular and voluminous correspondence they had succeeded in becoming part of the bric-à-brac in Tony's and Laura's lives.

'I can't imagine how we came to know them at all,' said Laura. 'But there they are, and we'll have to put up with them.'

All through the breakfast she had shot dazzling glances at Herbert and Lottie, and under this battery of radiance, the two felt themselves united in a conspiracy of adoration, and became friendly. Jo-Jo winked at Laura, and Laura winked at Tony and the drink flowed.

Lottie had asked for the salt in a mortified voice.

'You like salt, Miss Carstairs?' asked Herbert.

'Oh yes — may I call you Herbert? All my family are partial to salt. During the war, when we were living in Richmond, my mother used to have quite a thing about wasting salt. She used to hoard it, but unfortunately we discovered too late that the cupboard was damp. My mother was simply furious.'

'You are partial to condiments in general, Miss Carstairs?' asked Herbert, who did not ask might he call her 'Lottie'.

'Oh no, indeed,' replied Lottie. 'All my family are on the whole averse to condiments.' She was warming up.

'Except of course for salt — ever since my poor mother took ill after a week in Paris on those nasty French foods. The French, in *my* opinion, go in for an excessive use of condiments. My mother came out all over in spots, nasty red things they were. Ever since then we have preferred to eat with great simplicity — though of course we have our little fads. No, we like good plain fare. Plain — but good.'

Lottie's glass was refilled and Herbert grew bolder.

'You seem to be a very united family, Miss Carstairs.'

'Oh yes, we are indeed. Which is not to say that we are not individualistic as individuals — I mean — Oh dear, can one say that?'

But Laura's most vivid memory of her wedding was to be of her last sight of her friends and relations grouped in the doorway, or hanging from windows in snowy white lace curtains topped by fawn blinds, or scurrying to the gate with slack mouths and champagne-aerated *bons voyages.* She was to remember the two exactly parallel streams of tears running from her father's pouched eyes, and many times during the next month she was to see again with tremor of the heart Jo-Jo's lean greyhound body and her immutable Sienese face.

They drove away in a burst of sunlight and through the hurting glare Laura made an effort to take it all in, to stock-pile for the hungry days some details of the lucent present.

Her father and Jo-Jo were her childhood and young girlhood. Lottie, great swollen girl, was, if nothing else, a symbol of college days remoter now than the days of her fairy childhood. And there was Tony's Herbert, beaming in ivory at the dash and beauty of this couple who were his friends, and high in the house, very near the sky it seemed, three female cousins from God knows where, with long red hair hanging down their backs and voices like sea-birds, sang out 'I know my love' in clear gold August post-noon air.

Laura lay back in Tony's tobaccoed tweeds and was content to hold in her mind the light-stippled moments of her so successful wedding breakfast.

'Darling Aunt Jo-Jo,' she wrote, 'I feel a bit lonely sitting here without Tony who's gone to the café. I wonder sometimes if it's wise to be so dependent on another human being. You'll think I'm daft but without him I feel like I'd suddenly gone blind or lost my sense of touch.'

She managed to finish her letter before half-past ten. She fixed her make-up, threw on a light coat about her shoulders and, consciously throwing her head high, made down the Boulevard St Germain. The breeze was stirring up, played in her hair, and she threw her head higher still. She might have been of the *ancien régime*. Some yards ahead her guillotine lay ready. The stars were cold in the navy blue night.

At first she could not see Tony. Sara and Helen, two American divorcées, were alone at a table. Tony's usual cronies were getting on well without him. And then she saw him. He sat, away from the others, with a stranger, a young man of twenty or so. He had his glass raised, and he was smiling and he looked up happily at the cold stars. He saw Laura, and he waved. Her heart began to pound, she ran through the tables, stumbling over feet, almost overturning glasses and waiters, and came panting to Tony's table. She felt a tiny bubble of sweat on her left nostril.

'Sit down, darling,' said Tony. He did not get up, but the stranger did. 'This is a — Danish friend, Mr Holger Bjornson. Mr Bjornson doesn't speak English very well, but we're getting along nicely in German.'

'Hello,' she said simply. She had a ludicrous temptation to

167

cry out plaintively, 'But darling, you *know* I did French and Italian.' She bit her lip, and drank rapidly the cognac Tony had ordered. 'Jibber-jabber, jibber-jabber' she thought unjustly as she watched the Dane. She knew a little German, but clearly Tony was not concerned with keeping the conversation on her level. Soon she found herself smiling at jokes she didn't understand, and the smiles, she felt, did not always come in the right places. God, she thought, Tony's being damn rude to me. Yet he smiled continually and seemed unaware of any awkwardness. He burst into laughter at something the Dane said, and Laura asked curtly, 'Would you mind translating, please?'

She realized that he was drunk. His eyes glittered. His lips, always full, seemed to have thickened. But she was not prepared for what he said.

'Holger thinks it would be a good thing if you left us.'

Once said, it seemed inevitable. The knocking in her heart seemed familiar. Tony was still smiling. Holger looked at her curiously. It was a moment scooped out of time and place.

She got up. The Dane is very beautiful, she thought.

'You are go-ing, old girl?' he said in English.

'Yes,' she said, 'my husband will explain.' Even while she said it, she was ashamed of the stress she laid on the word 'husband'. She turned and walked over to Sara and Helen. The table was littered with charge-slips. They too had drunk well tonight.

'I saw honey,' said Sara. *'Garçon, trois gins à l'eau.'*

The waiter came. When he had gone, Sara spoke.

'I saw, honey, I saw. Drink your gin, honey.'

'Yes honey,' said Helen, 'drink your gin.'

Laura gulped her drink.

'It doesn't matter, honey,' said Sara, 'I've seen this kind of thing before.'

'What kind of thing?' she answered stupidly.

'Young princes,' said Sara. 'They come along and they're poison. I've seen it happen to the most ordinary decent men.'

The gin was working on top of the cognac. She wanted, absurdly, to sing. She thought of the three mad, red-haired cousins, flown with champagne, singing from the billowing

168

white curtains, 'I know my love . . .' There had been a young prince in college, in her French class. All the girls, and perhaps some of the boys, had been in love with him. The Prince of Denmark *à la tour abolie*. She began to cry, a childish, undignified sniffle.

Helen gave her a handkerchief. They had many more gins. Boys and girls walked down the pavement arm-in-arm. In the silver shadow of the Church of St Germain a couple embraced for minutes. Drunken American yells klaxoned over the buzz of the café. Out of the corner of her eye, Laura saw Tony and the Dane. Goodnight, sweet prince. *Puisque je retrouve un ami si fidèle* . . .

'*Encore trois gins à l'eau,*' said Sara. Laura drank and wept. The two women gave her handkerchiefs and told her to drink up. Sara had a wild look in her eyes, but remained placid. Helen breathed fast. It was one o'clock.

'Listen, honey,' said Sara gently, 'crying your eyes out won't do you any good. He'll probably come back to you. Most of them do. I was one of the unlucky ones.'

'He'll never come back,' she said.

'May I have the key, darling?' Tony was beside her. He swayed slightly.

'Why?'

'Oh, nothing. I just thought I'd turn in. And I promised Holger a night-cap.'

'Go to hell,' she said.

He lurched back to his table.

'Give him the key,' said Sara.

'No, I can't. I can't stand it.'

'Give it to him and see what happens.'

She would give it to him. She walked across to them, trying hard to stay erect and aloof. She laid the key on the table. But he hardly looked at it. Only the Dane looked at her with great spaniel eyes. As she walked back to Sara and Helen, she began to pray. Dear Mother, let him not leave me. Sacred Heart, let him come back to me. Saint Anthony, please help me. God please, please. Sacred Heart of Jesus, I put my trust in Thee.

'I had it for three years before he left me,' said Sara. To Laura's horror, Sara had begun to cry, soundlessly and

169

motionlessly, like a cow. And Helen was stroking Sara's hand with gentle cooing noises.

'Don't lose him,' said Sara suddenly. 'Go over to him and find him again.'

Laura did not move.

'Damn you, you silly bitch,' bellowed Sara. 'Don't lose him.'

There was a crash, the tinkle of falling glass, a flood of French invective. Tony had fallen from his chair. Laura leaped up and ran across to the little crowd that had gathered. He lay sheet-white and helpless while the Dane was tugging at his arm. Together they picked him up, a dead weight splayed between their sagging arms.

'Come along, darling,' she whispered. 'Come along.'

They propped him across to the taxi rank. The driver they found looked at her, pityingly. *'Trop bu,'* he muttered, *'trop bu, comme tous les Américains.'*

The Dane was furious. *'Il n'est pas Américain.* He is a descendant of kings.'

The Dane helped her to undress him. Tony muttered balderdash about changing-rooms in his stupor. His romantically sad lips contorted and spat. His film-star forehead was dripping. They could not manage to button his pyjama jacket or tie the string of his pyjama trousers, and Laura could not turn away her eyes from the black curly hair at the breast and pit of his torso.

'Do you want a drink?'

'Ah no, old girl,' said the Dane. 'But smile, you smile nicely, old girl.'

'I'm hardly in the humour for smiling.' She noticed that his skin was as fresh as a girl's. She leant forward and kissed him on the lips. Then she let him out. They had not spoken again. Towards dawn Tony dragged her into his arms.

Two days later, they left for Dublin.

Water from the Well

BRIAN POWER

Now that the Monsignor will never be able to come again, life will never be the same for Una and Eileen.

When I recognized the envelope on the hall carpet last Wednesday, I realized at once that the news must be serious. My sisters do not write for reasons of courtesy or social obligation. The letter, in Eileen's liberal-sized handwriting, scarcely covered one side of the single ruled page. They had received word from a priest in the States that Monsignor Tom had taken a stroke. He was now in a wheelchair, semi-paralysed, they said. But he had been hale and hearty to a good old age and, even though they would miss his visit in September a great deal, welcome be God's holy will.

On Saturday morning I drove out from Galway through Gort and Ennis to take the car ferry from Killimer to Tarbert. The introduction a few years ago of the ferry across the Shannon made it possible to cut the journey to my old homestead by well over an hour. This was the first time it occurred to me to take advantage of it.

It was a long time since I had felt any sense of hurry about arriving. My wife, Isabelle, a Galway city girl with an Arts degree, finds it hard to accept Una and Eileen as real. After my parents died, it became my custom to drive down to the farm with Isabelle the first weekend every June. We would stay in Tralee overnight before going on after lunch to my sisters' place, where we would aim to arrive an hour or two before tea. That meant we could leave in time to get a good night's rest in the hotel in preparation for an early morning start back to Galway.

Isabelle likes things to be neatly worked out like that, and I must confess I have grown accustomed to an orderly life myself. Besides, I reasoned, my sisters had enough work to do without putting up guests into the bargain. The arrangement, or so I imagined, was mutually satisfactory. Our visit, I could safely pride myself, was for them one of the great occasions of the year. Not *the* great occasion, of course. The great occasion was the fortnight's stay made with them every September by the Monsignor. Right Reverend and Vicar-General and all.

There was half an hour to wait for the ferry when I reached Killimer. I gazed across at the powerhouse chimney and lighthouse of Tarbert on the opposite shore of the estuary while my mind travelled back over my sisters' anecdotes concerning the Monsignor. Although Father Tom , as my mother always called him, was her youngest brother, my only contact with him for many years had been an exchange of greeting cards at Christmas. For my sisters, he was the pivot around which life revolved. Isabelle and I discovered on our visits to the farm that the lapse of nine months since the Monsignor's vacation there never erased from their minds every detail of his activities and conversation. For a fortnight the house had sprung to life. Neighbours and old friends came from miles around to drink tea in the mornings or whiskey in the evenings, card parties played one-hundred-and-tens until the wee hours, and guns roared death in the afternoons for duck on the moor or rabbits in the high fields on the mountainside.

'It's just like everything used to be in the old days,' my sisters would say, their eyes bright, their voices raised, exuding an animation which only this one topic could elicit.

What could ever replace the excitement of all this?

Maiden sisters in middle age, I began to realize, could become quite a problem. Too late now to question the accepted scale of values which, in my family in County Kerry, decreed that sons be sent away for higher education while daughters were trusted to look out for suitable husbands for themselves. Packed off to study accountancy in Galway at the same time as Una and Eileen were feeding pigs and taking in hay, I never remember experiencing embarrassment or shame. My parents' plans went astray, just the same. It was the boys who married and roamed, and that without much delay, while the two girls, plodding faithfully about their chores, didn't seem to have much time to search for husbands. Desolate and uneconomic, the little farm was no Mecca for pleasure-hunters who might travel back to their native haunts with a bride or two in tow.

The ferry came, sleighing its way slowly across the river. Only a few cars waited to crawl down the ramp and take their places on the plane of the boat which shook and purred like a washing machine as the engines began to rev. Following the example of the occupants of the other cars, I ascended one of the twin decks to get a view of the river. The heavy drizzle soon drove most of us back to the shelter of our vehicles. Not that it mattered. The ferry had barely begun to pick up speed, ploughing the knobbly wavelets, when it had to slow again approaching journey's end. Somehow, it gave me a feeling of strangeness to find myself crossing water to reach my sisters, as if the experience emphasized the width of the gulf which separated my world from theirs. I began to wish that, even though it was only a few weeks since our June visit, I had persuaded Isabelle to accompany me. With her by my side, there would be no need to attempt to bridge the gap. She would chatter away about bridge parties, local drama, and the relative merits and demerits of the various secondary schools of Galway. Back in the hotel bedroom, she would say as she removed her hat, 'Poor Una and Eileen, they're sweet but they have so little to say. All they can talk about is the Monsignor.'

Would they talk about anything else tonight? Would the fact that the Monsignor could not come in September after all reveal to them the fundamental loneliness of their lives, perhaps unleash a stream of confidences? The thought depressed me. What could be done? I had shot off on this errand of mercy with the intention of brightening up things a little for my sisters, but only now did I begin to worry for fear they might make more demands on me than I was prepared for.

I decided to stop at a Grade A hotel for lunch, even ordered a half-bottle of white Spanish wine to relax my nerves, jangled by the prospect of being obliged to meet Una and Eileen on a more intimate footing than any that had existed between us since my childhood. Gradually, the restaurant fare restored my morale. Sipping a coffee and liqueur, I stretched my legs, savouring the peacefulness of

173

unaccustomed solitude. In the rear garden towards which my table was facing thin, willowy trees upheld by staves drooped leaved heads before the breeze. Along the length of the stone wall backing the garden flitted the gleaming blue helmet of a motor-cyclist on the road beyond. I rose to go. The truth would have to be faced. The Monsignor would not be coming to Ireland again and my sisters had discovered a void in their lives. Of course, I needn't have concerned myself. Perhaps I shouldn't have. But what was so difficult, after all, about making a gesture? Surely that was not beyond the range of my generosity? Perish the thought.

Sitting at the plain deal kitchen table an hour later, while Una and Eileen clucked and chucked about my comfort, I almost laughed at my fears. Nothing had changed, surely? Solemnly Una produced freshly baked brown bread and apple tart, cutting large slices and laying them on plates bedecked with paper doilies. She did most of the talking, as befitted her matriarchal position in the family, enquiring about Isabelle and the children, the journey down, the state of my health. Her long fair hair, now turning grey, streeled about her shoulders like an untidy schoolgirl's.

Eileen wears hers short and closecropped, peers like an owl through cheap hornrimmed glasses, interjects occasional brief phrases like 'surely' or ''tis true for you' to show that she is mindful of my presence. Secure in the knowledge of all that is about to happen, I watch Eileen take the pail from its hanger on the back of the door, then plod out patiently, bramble marks red above knee-high wellingtons, setting off to the well for pure spring water for the tea. Although they have taps installed with the new sink unit, my sisters would not dream of using water from the tap to make tea for a visitor.

While I wait, I tell Una about the novelty of the car ferry trip.

'Sure, 'tis wonderful the things they think of nowadays,' she says. 'It must be very convenient.'

Soon Eileen is back to fill the kettle and set it on the gas ring. Carefully, she takes the big earthenware teapot with the blue stripe from its hook on the dresser, then stands hugging it between the palms of her hands waiting for the kettle to boil. Meanwhile Una hacks handsome slices of cured ham, pours thick creamy milk from a covered bucket into a jug, begins to tell me about the farm work, how she and Eileen got on better with the dehorning when the electric dehorner was introduced than any of the men in neighbouring farms.

'There's not much we can't do that they can do,' she boasts quietly. 'If only we had a man for a bit of the heavy work, we'd be well away, so we would.'

As Una, at a signal from Eileen, warms the teapot and wets the tea, I lay into the meal as if I were a boy again. Darky, the new terrier, and Con, the aging sheepdog, draw close beneath the table, hoping for scraps. For half an hour I am unfaithful to Isabelle, eating and reminiscing, reflecting at the back of my mind how I might now be living in all this peace, the man about the place who, in return for being monarch of all he surveyed, would only have to do the little bit of heavy work that proved to be beyond my sisters' womanly energies.

At last I sit back contentedly, pull out a packet of cigarettes and offer them to Una and Eileen. Sometimes they accept in honour of the occasion. Tonight, however, they shake their heads in unison.

'Sure enough we used to smoke the odd one,' Una explains, 'But when we found they weren't ricomminded, we decided to keep away from them altogether. There's no sinse in it when they're not ricomminded.'

Then Eileen stretches across the table, takes a cigarette and says daringly, 'Sure maybe I will after all, just this once, for the sake of company.'

Watching her puff cautiously at the poisonous weed, I wondered to discover how fond I was of my two sisters. I had almost forgotten. Hating to break the spell, yet fearing that I might be drawn too far into the past, I decided that I had better raise the subject of the Monsignor.

'So Monsignor Tom is not so well.'

Una nodded gravely.

'That's why we sent for you.'

So they took it for granted that I would come, I thought, and felt glad that I had not disappointed them. Certainly they said nothing in the letter to suggest that I should come,

175

they simply trusted in me to understand. Even with the pleasure, alarm crept back. What had they in mind? Why should they have wanted me to come?

'It was a great thing for us knowing that he would be here every year,' Una continued. 'There were all sorts of little things he would do that we never got round to. Like last September when he shot a few stray cats that had been bothering us, gone wild they were, and then he shot old Barney, you remember the terrier was here last time you came. He was very old but Eileen and me would never have had the heart to shoot him. The Monsignor got Darky for us instead so that we wouldn't miss Barney. We're not much good with the gun, that's one thing you need a man for. We were only saying it was a pity he didn't shoot Con as well, it will have to be done soon, mind you, and Eileen and me wouldn't have the heart.'

For one panic-stricken moment it occurred to me that they had wanted me for this express purpose, me who had forgotten what it was even like to live on an isolated farm.

'He was great with the gun, the Monsignor,' corroborated Eileen. 'But even at that itself we had talked a few times this last year or two of what we have in mind, what we wanted to see you about. Nothing more than to talk now, mind you. There's no hurry in the world, now.'

More perceptive than Una, she had divined that her sister's words had frightened me a little. Perplexed, I bided my time. Whatever it was, they would come out with it in their own way. Already Una was off at a tangent and it was several minutes before she returned to the point.

'What we were thinking was how we do need a man about the place. We'll be needing one soon anyway. We're not getting younger. I'm not far off fifty myself, so we'd better be thinking about it now even if it might take a little bit of time.'

I looked with affection at her witch's hair and thought, surely she's not thinking of marriage? Not far off fifty! Fifty-three would be more like it.

Eileen took the initiative quite suddenly.

'You know the McCormick's old house that's on our land? In the second field across?'

Una said, 'That's what it is. We were thinking how we might find a man that would like to live in it in return for a bit of work about the place. He could be any age, fifty to sixty maybe because the young men might find it too quiet in these parts.'

Eileen was studying my reactions, I could feel her eyes boring into my mind.

'It's a fine house,' she said. 'It only needs a few things done with it. Any man wouldn't find it too hard to fix it up.'

I nodded, remembering that last year I had gone into the house to take a look round. The timbers were rotting, the slates falling off the roof. It hadn't been occupied for years since the last of the McCormicks had cleared off to America, selling the house and a couple of fields for a song to my sisters. There was no water, no electricity. The man who might take it would hardly be fit to do a day's work. Indeed, the most miserable tramp would scarcely want to live there, for he would be better off in a city hostel. Perhaps a poet or a hermit . . . but in the new Ireland even poets and hermits tended to believe that they could operate more efficiently with all mod cons. I said none of this, concentrating on assuming an expression of cautious interest as my sisters waxed enthusiastic about the difference it would make to life on the farm to have a man about the place.

At last Una said, 'So what we thought was how you might ask around among all those fine people you know in Galway if they could recommend someone who might like the house. We couldn't afford to pay him, of course, but we'd give him all his meals here and all he'd have to do would be a few of the heavy jobs. Not all that much at all, because there's not much we can't do that a man could do. Just it would be a comfort to know he was there if we ever needed him. There's times now one or other of us mightn't be in the best of form, although mostly we have our health, thank God. Then again, it's getting more lonely in these parts than it used to be and you never know who might be prowling around out from the cities and the towns.'

It troubled me to hear them go on and on and feel powerless to find the miracle they were seeking. When I retired for the night, I made up my mind that I would bring the pair of them off for the day on Sunday. I would drive them to Shannon airport where the planes would not fail to throw them into paroxysms of awe and delight, then give them lunch in some discreet restaurant where they would be made to feel like royalty without being overwhelmed by pomp. I would make this a weekend they would remember . . . but where could I or anybody else find the man of their dreams? That he did not exist I was certain. They could recall the days of their childhood when such men wandered the countryside in search of work, men who would work their hearts out for a bed to lie on and a bite to eat, men who had learned what it was to wonder each morning where they would sleep that night. They would remember, too, that many of these men had a nobility and strength of character all their own, and they would be happy to go to bed each evening in the knowledge that such a man slept only two fields away to guard them from all danger and from the ultimate loneliness of unprotected womanhood. That they had not come across any of these willing spalpeens for quite some years did not, apparently, daunt them. Their brother in Galway would search one of them out; they had surely moved on rather than disappeared. Oh innocence, I groaned, and in my slumbers I argued with the shades of my father and my mother about the future of my sisters, something that would never have occurred to me to do when my parents were alive.

Sunday went according to plan. Una and Eileen in flower-patterned frocks demurely licked ice-cream sundaes in a Limerick café, blessed themselves as they skipped in thrilled ecstasy to see the jet exploding away from Shannon, and never once reverted to the subject of their decision to seek a man about the farm. Eileen even took the wheel for a few miles on the way back — it is she who drives the tractor and the old Ford which she never uses save strictly on business. She drove my heavy car with her head low over the steering-wheel, her foot barely tapping the accelerator, yet without the hint of a suggestion that she might not be equal to the task.

"'Tis fortunate Eileen has such good driving sense,' said Una. 'Not that I wouldn't be able to manage the car if I had to, but as long as one of us can do it there's no need to worry. With the way people speed along the roads these days I'm as happy not to have to worry.'

When we got back to the house, I settled into an armchair while the teatime ritual went into motion. I was fully prepared for a resumption of the previous night's discussion. When I finally moved back to the armchair from the table after a hearty meal, however, Una began to talk about Monsignor Tom's last visit.

'Little did we think it would be his last, and him so hale and hearty. Where are those photographs he sent, Eileen? Eileen took some of himself with his camera.'

Then, as Eileen rummaged in a drawer of the dresser, Una added, 'I suppose the only way we could see him again now would be for the two of us to fly to America. But sure even if we could afford it itself, the two of us could hardly go together and one of us on her own would surely get lost in a big place like that.'

From then on it was photographs and memories. The smiling teddybear features of the Monsignor surmounting buttoned stock and alpaca jacket recurred in technicolour splendour in Irish holiday settings. In other photographs taken at parish ceremonies he was more exotically clad, surrounded by happy altar boys, junior clergy and smartly uniformed sisters. The photographs exhausted the night. We went to bed without any mention being made of the need for a man about the place.

On Monday I had an early breakfast so that it was only eight o'clock when I got into the car to head back to Galway. The dew on the grass smelt sweet, the clouds hung low overhead, the dogs leaped around the wheels barking excitedly. Una and Eileen directed me with flapping, shooing hand movements as I reversed into a gateway to get the car pointed down the boreen.

Only as I leaned out of the window to give a final wave and salutation did Una say, 'Don't forget now to enquire about a suitable man for the McCormick house. There's no hurry in it, but maybe you'll come down when you get a chance and we can discuss it again.'

'When we see you, sure you can tell us if there's any news,' added Eileen.

Keeping the smile fixed firmly on my face, murmuring that I would not forget to enquire around, I drove carefully down the narrow lane, the sides of the car brushing the hedges and snapping the protruding briars until I reached the road. Before I had travelled a mile, rain pelted against the windscreen, forcing me to concentrate on my driving. Only with the swish of the wipers the thought repeated itself again and again: are they really serious? Do they think I am a magician or what?

In the car ferry once again I felt that sensation of passing from one world into another. As we crossed the channel, rain streaming down the car windows made the trip seem like an underwater voyage, a couple of car aerials ahead of me like the antennae of submarines. Thoughtfully, I lit a cigarette and stared at my image in the small mirror.

'You fool,' I told myself, 'how little you understand women.'

For it had begun to dawn on me that Una and Eileen, deprived of their main prop in life, felt compelled to make sure of substituting another. Perhaps they really believed that it would be possible to find a handyman to live in the old McCormick house and give a little assistance on the farm. Perhaps not. This was not what mattered. What mattered was that there should be somebody towards whom they could turn for regular reassurance that they were not entirely abandoned and alone in the world . . . That was why they had wanted me to come.

Isabelle may find it hard to understand, although I know that she will make a gallant effort to do so. Come what may, I must go down to the old homestead again very soon. Just to talk about the possibility of getting a man to stay about the place. And after that quite soon again. And again. We will talk for ever about a man for the McCormick house, although we will never find one.

800327

BEST IRISH SHORT STORIES
7.95

800327

BEST IRISH SHORT STORIES
7.95

SS   89

FEB 2 9 1996